THE FERAL FAE'S HUMAN

WILD HUNT 2

LOLA GLASS

Cover by Francesca Michelon
https://www.merrybookround.com/

To the books and people who make dark days a little brighter.

ONE

MY MUSIC PLAYED LOUDLY ENOUGH to drown out the sounds of the men fighting outside. The northern wall of my bedroom was covered in wet paint; its newest mural was a gruesome picture of fire, hellhounds, and death.

That was all I saw when I closed my eyes, after all.

Myself, burning.

Priel, my fake fae mate, dying.

All the hounds in this damn world, turning to ash.

And me, at the center of them.

It wasn't any kind of future-sight, as far as I knew. My brain was just really damn twisted.

There was a knock at my door.

"I'm not hungry," I snarled at whoever was there.

I felt bad for snarling, but not bad enough to chill. If they came in, they'd see the evidence of my dreams and nightmares all over the walls. Some of them knew that I painted, but most of them didn't. I didn't really care whether they knew or not, as long as they didn't see how messed up my brain was. They'd probably kick me out of the Stronghold, and I was not interested in trying to deal with this messed up world of single fae dudes alone.

The fae had no women, so they wanted us—ex-humans that they'd dragged through a portal from Earth because we were stupid enough to make a wish to escape our world on the one night of the year that the fae dudes could break through.

There was a loud crack, and then my locked door swung open.

I was on my feet in an instant, my eyes burning as I snarled at the person in the doorway.

But it wasn't someone who would fear my fire.

It was the hellhound who haunted my dreams—and not just the nightmares. If I had one more sex dream about the bastard, I was going to burn my bed. On *purpose* this time.

"*Get out*," I roared at him.

"No can do, little flame." Priel (pronounced 'preel') crossed the room, stalking toward me like a damn predator.

I didn't step back. I knew better than to run from someone who could take me down. "Don't fucking touch me."

"Sorry, love. Got to get some rest." With that, he grabbed me by the waist, threw me over his shoulder, and took off out the door.

Fucking hell, I was screwed.

He shifted into his bear-like hellhound form as he made his way out of the Stronghold, moving too fast for any of the other women to stop me, even if they'd wanted to.

I doubted that they wanted to, though. We weren't on great terms. Or good terms. Or even... terms.

Yeah, no.

Those chicks weren't going to rescue my grumpy, hostile ass.

My fingers dug into Priel's thick, fiery fur. It looked like it was made entirely out of flames, but the fire didn't burn me. Honestly it felt kind of nice on my skin.

Not that I'd ever admit it.

"Put me down!" I yelled at the fae guy, as he sprinted into the forest a hell of a lot faster than I'd realized he could move. My clothes—a long-sleeved shirt with a high neckline and long, loose pants, all made out of black fabric—didn't burn away somehow, so maybe he could control whether his fire was hot or not.

We barreled past about a million other fae guys as we went— many of which turned and started sprinting after us.

The Wild Hunt guys were keeping the other men away from me and the other ex-human ladies by pretending to be somewhere along the mating process with us. Unfortunately, that didn't stop the other fae from challenging them to fights. And more fights. And more damn fights.

If we'd actually been deep in the mating process, our scents would've started intertwining, so me and the other girls had to stay inside for the most part.

That wasn't abnormal for us, though.

And considering that now, the other fae could see me and smell me—and probably reach me—I knew everything was about to blow up in our faces.

"Hurry!" I yelled at Priel, gripping his fur tighter.

He didn't speed up, but a few more minutes passed, and I realized none of the fae chasing us were gaining on us. If anything, they were getting a little further behind us.

Priel kept running, and the distance between us and them started to widen.

And eventually, I couldn't see any other fae on the horizon.

It was just me, and him.

HE SLOWED as we approached some jagged-looking rocks. I expected him to stop and let me off before we reached wherever we were going, but all of the sudden, he dove downward, and the ground seemed to drop out from underneath us.

A yelp escaped me as we plummeted into some kind of hole.

He landed smoothly, and I slowly lifted my face off of his back so I could look around the area. It seemed to be some kind of cave, and thanks to the magic coursing through my veins, I could see in the darkness of the room without a problem.

Before I got a good look at anything, Priel started to shift, and I flung myself off his back. I collided with the hard, smooth stone floor and instinctively made a pained noise even though it didn't really hurt.

A pair of gigantic hands grabbed me around the waist, plucking me off the ground and setting me on my feet.

"What are you doing?" The bastard sounded amused.

I stepped further away from him. "I'd rather not end up plastered to your human body, considering you *abducted* me."

"There's nothing *human* about me, female." His eyes reminded me of my own transformed orbs. The reddish-gold scared me every damn time I looked in the mirror.

I couldn't stop my gaze from sliding quickly down his body.

The man was a fucking work of art. He was massive, thick everywhere and much bigger than any human man could possibly be. Red, black, and gold tattoos covered almost every inch of his skin, and since all he had on were a pair of colorful shorts, there was plenty of skin showing.

I hadn't actually been calling him human; I wasn't that moronic. Priel couldn't have passed for a human if he tried, and he definitely didn't.

But it had annoyed him, so I just shrugged a shoulder and stepped to the side, intending to check out the cave he was holding me in.

He had made it very clear that he wasn't interested in being anything other than fake mates, so I knew he wouldn't try to feel me up or anything. That removed pretty much all of the fear that should've been involved in the abduction.

His voice followed me as I walked away from him. "I haven't slept more than an hour or two in months. My pack will keep the other fae away while we're here, so I can rest. When I've recovered, I'll take you back to the Stronghold."

I didn't respond, my eyebrows lifting as I took in the walls of the cave.

They looked like the walls of my room.

Minus all of the death, of course.

And the hidden bits and pieces of my sex dreams featuring the hellhound who wanted to keep things very, very platonic between us.

I'd been dreaming about him long before I drew his name and ended up fake-mated to him. I had tried to convince the other women to consider letting us choose our fake mates, too—or at least let us each have a veto to make sure we didn't end up with, oh, the fae we'd been sex-dreaming about for a year.

It hadn't worked, and of course, I drew the flaming bastard's name.

My gaze moved slowly over the images on the walls. Most of them were gorgeous landscapes—renditions of Vevol's beach, of its trees, of its mountains. Many of them featured the flaming bear-wolf creatures that the fae called hellhounds.

I was one of said hellhounds, though I had managed to stop myself from shifting thus far.

"You haven't said anything," Priel growled at me.

I silently flipped him my middle finger.

A low chuckle rumbled his chest. I wished I was pressed up against him, so I could feel that rumble, and then cursed myself silently for wishing that.

"Wake me up when you get hungry."

He stalked away, and I heard the rustle of blankets somewhere off to my right.

I'd never dreamed about us being together in this cave before, obviously. But based on the home I had imagined us together in, I wasn't at all surprised by how sparsely-furnished Priel's place was.

All of the walls were covered in paintings, but otherwise all he had was a huge bed, a shelf and table that were loaded with their world's version of art supplies, a bathroom, and a small kitchen.

I heard Priel's breathing even out a minute later.

My stomach clenched unpleasantly.

Clearly, he was nowhere near as attracted to me as I was to him. I didn't think there was a chance in hell that I'd be able to fall asleep in the same room as him.

Since I had nothing else to do, I slowly walked the perimeter of the room, checking out the paintings. I noticed a smallish hellhound in every one, and figured Priel had just painted himself a little smaller than he really was to make the landscape shine.

I wandered over to the art table after I'd studied all of the paintings.

There was an assload of paint, and something within me was settled by that. None of the tubes of paint seemed to have been opened recently, and they were all extremely clean and well-taken-care-of. The first fact was probably my fault, considering the bastard had been fighting off other fae to keep them from trying to hook up with me. But the second one made me curious.

Priel definitely wasn't a slob, if his living space was any kind of evidence. I... sort of was. It wasn't that I tried to make messes, or enjoyed having a messy living space. When it started to feel cluttered, I would move things.

I just wasn't a fan of the typical organization method that involved throwing everything into bins or lining it up on shelves. Leaving things exactly where I would use them next was far more logical to me.

My eyes moved over a massive stack of what sort of resembled sketch pads. The papers were all connected by some type of vine, which I found kind of fascinating. I'd never been great at sketching, preferring to figure shit out while I was painting it and just throw a little black or white on there if I needed a reset button.

Paint worked with my hands and mind; pens and paper usually did not.

That was the real factor, I supposed.

My eyes landed on a set of strange equipment next, and my forehead wrinkled.

It looked just like the strange, magical tattoo gun I had dreamed about Priel using on both of us at different times. Not *all* of my dreams of us together were sex dreams; just most of them.

There was a sharp bit at the end, and a bunch of small jars of paint around it. I picked it up carefully, studying it.

Though I'd seen Priel hold it to my skin in my dreams, I had no idea how it was supposed to work, or even how my subconscious had invented something that actually existed.

The needle would need to go up and down, wouldn't it? To break the skin?

Hmm.

I unscrewed the lid on a jar of silver paint and then rolled one of my sleeves up just enough to expose one of the bruise-like burns that covered much of my skin. When I came to Vevol, I'd had an assload of scars. And when my magic settled a few weeks after I'd arrived, I'd woken up on fire one day.

The flames hadn't hurt, but my clothes had been roasted, and all of my many scars had morphed into terrible-looking purplish-black patches that looked like a mix between bruises and burns.

I kept them covered so I wouldn't scare any of the other women... and maybe just in case a fae guy came to the door for me.

Preferably a blond, inked-up fae guy.

It hadn't happened since the beginning of my time in Vevol, which was my fault. I knew it was my fault.

But I still kind of wished the men would come.

That *he* would come.

Or at least, I *had* wished that, until the fae men realized that the mating bond could form over time. Then they'd started flooding the Stronghold. And I didn't know how to talk to them, or how to consider them, so I just... didn't.

But I'd always seen the way my parents loved each other. They were shitty people, honestly. Good to me and my older sister, but shitty people.

None of my scars had been their fault. At least, not directly or intentionally.

Now, none of my bruise-burn-things were.

And damn, I missed them.

My chest was tight at the thought of it.

There was no way back to Earth, though. And if I had found a way back, I eventually would've regretted going. My parents' business would've been unavoidable, and I would've ended up doing shitty things myself.

At least I had escaped before that happened.

I NEEDED to force my thoughts back to the present, so I dunked the tip of the magical tattoo gun into the ink and then lowered it to my skin. I didn't know what I'd create, but then again, I rarely did.

Biting my lip in preparation, I carefully stuck the tip into my skin.

A sharp flash of pain followed—and blood gushed over the small cut as I lifted it back out, muttering curses under my breath.

My eyes stung a bit.

Whew, that hurt.

"What the hell?" Priel's tired, grumpy ass growled from the bed. "Why do I smell blood?"

"I'm fine," I shot back, setting the tattoo gun back down and easing my sleeve over the discolored patch of skin again. When I pressed the black fabric to the wound, it soaked up the blood quickly.

Maybe I was bleeding more than I'd realized.

Heavy footsteps sounded on the ground, and my stomach clenched.

Fuck, I was terrible at talking to Priel. I didn't know what to say, or how to say it, or how not to sound like a complete bitch. Or if I even *wanted* to not sound like a complete bitch.

He was gorgeous.

And I was... not.

I mean, my face was fine. I'd never really been allowed to talk to guys, so I didn't have many interactions to base that idea off of, but I hadn't been told I was hideous or anything. My parents had homeschooled me and my sister, because going to school would've been too dangerous for us given my parents' questionable life and business decisions.

They were sort of... mafia.

Okay, not sort of.

They *were* mafia.

They'd even arranged my sister and I into those damn mafia-family marriages you read about in romance books. My sister was happy with her man, but I didn't know what those authors were smoking, because my experience sure as hell didn't resemble a romance book.

I'd ended up jumping out of a moving car to save my own life before the supposed marriage. Then, I'd spent a month in the hospital recovering from said jump a few days later, when my parents realized I'd been alone in the damn forest for multiple days and sent someone to find me.

The PTSD was a nightmare. Therapy had helped a little, but that and my parents' overprotectiveness had been the reason behind my wish on a bunch of birthday candles for a fresh start.

That wish—and having a birthday on what was apparently Winter Solstice—got me dragged to Vevol.

I hadn't wanted to leave my family, or even my life. I just...

Well, I didn't know what I wanted.

I'd been in Vevol for well over a year and a half, and yet I still hadn't figured that shit out.

Maybe I never would.

At least I had paint.

But anyway, my body wasn't art. Not the way Priel's was. I wasn't nice to look at; I could imagine his potential cringe vividly assuming he saw the patch of bleeding, bruised-looking skin, and tugged my sleeve down further.

He walked up to me and plucked the tattoo gun from my hand. The tip of it caught on fire, and my blood burned off of it quickly before he set the tool back down on the table, exactly where I had picked it up from. "What are you doing?

"I was trying to give myself a tattoo. Couldn't figure out how that thing worked." I tossed a hand toward the tool. "On Earth, they have motors."

At least, I thought they did. I didn't know anything about them, honestly.

"Giving a tattoo requires altering a person's magic. You don't break the skin with that," he grumbled at me, grabbing my hand.

His sudden grip surprised me. It took me a minute to process the warm, comforting feel of his skin on mine.

Before I recovered enough to tug my hand away, he peeled my sleeve up my arm.

And then stared down at my patch of skin—and the already-healing cut—for way too long.

I tried to tug my hand from his grip again, but it tightened around my wrist.

"What is this?" He finally looked up at me.

"Don't worry about it," I snarled.

He still wouldn't let go, so I shoved my knee up toward his crotch. The bastard caught it deftly, and I swore when he held me by the arm and knee both.

"Where and when did you get this?" Priel's eyes were fiery, as always. The color wasn't always so bright and intense, but fire blossomed within the orbs whenever he got all riled up, and I seemed to rile him up almost constantly.

"Let go of me," I shot back.

He released my knee, but stepped closer to me, his eyes dipping back to my forearm. "I need an answer, North. This kind of marking is something we call Vevol's Brand. She only brands those who can tap into her magic on a deep, dangerous level." He *finally* let go of my arm and stepped back.

My eyes flew open wide when he stripped his pants off, turning his back to me and flashing a gorgeous, tight, tattooed ass in my direction.

Shit.

Holy shit.

His finger pointed to the back of one of his thighs, and my eyes finally unglued from his butt long enough to see what he was pointing to.

A large, purplish-black bruise-burn that he hadn't touched with any ink. It had become a part of his body's artwork, blending in with everything else, but I had seen enough of them to know it was the same as mine.

A *Vevol's Brand*.

"I caught fire shortly after I figured out how to break through the veil between our worlds to bring women through to Vevol, and this appeared," he said, his voice low as he looked at me intensely over his shoulder, studying me. "When did yours appear?"

Oh, shit.

He thought I only had the one brand.

Honesty would probably be best, but if those things were supposed to be rare, then I couldn't just tell him I had dozens.

"A few weeks after I was brought here." I tugged my sleeve back down my arm, ignoring the awful feeling of the damp, bloody fabric dragging over my skin.

His eyes narrowed. "Before or after the last time I brought you supplies?"

Did he actually remember doing that?

I had been pretty damn sure he thought I was the most uninteresting person ever. He hadn't even bothered flirting with me, like he did the other women.

That didn't stop me from having sex dreams about him.

"Before."

If he questioned how perfectly I remembered those times and our interactions in particular, I'd make another attempt at kneeing him in the balls.

"You should've told me." His words were nearly a snarl.

My snapped response came out before I could think it through. "Why the hell would I do that? The other girls got pretty magical tattoos; I got awful-looking burns. And you were *far* from interested in me or my life."

His eyes narrowed. "Burns?"

The emphasis he put on the "s" made me curse silently.

I glared back at him, literally biting my tongue to stop myself from saying things I would regret.

"Where's your other one?" he demanded.

"None of your damn business. And if you try to strip me to find it, I will scream until one of the other fae shows up and kills you for *hurting* me."

His eyes burned with fury, and he grabbed his shorts off the ground, turning as he yanked them up his body. "I would never fucking do that."

"Then back off." I spun around, stalking to the bathroom and shutting myself inside. The door locked behind me, and I collapsed against it. My eyes were stinging, and my body was shaking.

My burn-bruises were *brands*?

Special markings that somehow represented Vevol?

What the hell did that mean?

Two

WHEN I EVENTUALLY CALMED MYSELF down enough to step back out into the room, I found Priel sitting on the edge of the bed, tapping his foot harshly on the floor. I'd come up with a plan that would get me away from the bastard. It wasn't an ideal plan, but it was a hell of a lot better than spending the next few days alone with him in his home.

His gaze jerked up to me as I stepped out, and darkened when he saw me.

"I've decided to face the rest of the fae and look for an actual mate to end the fighting," I told him bluntly. "Thanks for trying to protect me, but I'm done with this whole fake-mate shitshow."

Forcing myself to remain calm, I crossed the room until I was standing right below the hole we'd fallen into to get into the place.

When I eyed the wall, I realized there were handholds and footholds of sort.

Of course the fiery bastard had to climb a literal rock wall to get out of his house.

"You can't do that." Priel's fingers wrapped around my wrist as I reached toward the wall.

I flashed him a glare. "Why the hell not?"

"Because if anyone sees a glimpse of either of those brands, you'll become worth a lot more than any of the other women."

I blinked.

Women were the most valuable thing in Vevol. There were only twenty of us, to *hundreds* of men. And while we weren't treated like objects, or property, or money, we could get almost anything we wanted just by batting our eyes at the men.

"Why would that make me *worth more*?"

"Vevol branded you. She *chose* you. Your power will be far more intense than any of the other women. There are only two of us male fae with brands, North. I discovered and opened the portal to the human world. The unseelie king turns his half of the world into an icy mess to enforce the borders between our territories."

Shit.

So the markings were even worse than I thought.

That sounded like just my luck.

Priel's gaze was steady as he stared at me. "You need to learn how to access whatever power Vevol gave you when she branded you, so you can protect yourself, before you even consider choosing a mate."

I scoffed and pulled my wrist from his grip.

He let me go, that time.

I argued, "It sounds like what I *need* to do is choose a mate before word gets out about my magic."

His eyes burned hotter. "Our supposed connection will protect you. None of the other fae will take you from me; they know that doing so could convince me not to open the portal between our worlds, and they're desperate to find their other halves."

I tossed a hand toward him. "They don't even believe that we're together. If they did, we would've had sex by now, and they wouldn't be challenging you. Right?"

His jaw clenched.

Yeah, I had thought so.

The only thing we had done to create the beginning of our "mate bond" was a quick peck on the lips. It had been awkward as hell, and I'd shut myself away in my room for a month afterward so I wouldn't have to see him again.

Seeing him, kissing him...

Well, my unconscious self already had a crush on the guy. The sex in my dreams was unreal, and there wasn't a chance in hell that it could ever happen like that in real life, even if Priel was interested in me.

Which he was not, nor had he ever been.

I went on. "Right now, they're all chasing me because they don't think I've made a real connection. If I can make that happen with someone and my scent actually changes, would most of the fae back off?"

The fierce clench of his jaw told me that my hunch was right.

"If these brands are as important as you claim, and I'm really in danger because of them, then I need to act. Right?"

"Right. But there are many ways to *act*." Priel ground the words out.

"Well, I've already made up my mind." I spun around, stalking toward the rock wall. My toes found the first hold, and I pulled myself up a few inches before his hands latched onto my waist.

He plucked me off the wall and set me on my feet, before stepping up close. Our chests pressed together, and I inhaled sharply at the contact.

"The fae already believe I'm pursuing you, at least somewhat. They know that our connection has begun to form, even if they don't truly believe we have a relationship. If safety is what you seek, *I* am the answer. Not another male." His voice was a low, harsh growl.

Maybe if he'd been asking because he wanted me, I would've agreed.

Maybe if he'd told me he was attracted to me, or called me his, I would've kissed the hell out of him.

Because he didn't, I ignored the flashes from my dreams that rolled through my mind with his ideas.

I opened my mouth to tell him to back off, but then his hips trapped me to the wall.

My mind went blank when I felt his erection against my belly.

"My pack doesn't believe I've claimed you because my scent isn't on your body. We change that, and we'll earn the pack's belief. They'll spread the word faster than I ever could."

"How would we do that?" I argued. "I'm not having sex with you."

"Of course not," he scoffed.

My defenses rose, and I tried to shove him away from me.

He didn't budge. "Sunny and Teris merged their scents slightly by kissing more intensely. We'll do the same."

"Like hell we will. Step away from me, now," I bit out.

He took the tiniest step back.

His erection was still trapped against me, but I forced myself to remember that he wasn't attracted to me; he was attracted to the fact that I was a woman.

"I'm not doing this," I told him, forcing my voice to remain steady.

His nostrils flared, and hot anger burned in his eyes.

He did step back, though.

Finally, I could breathe.

"My pack lives close by. I spoke with them; they're keeping other fae away while I rest. They're trustworthy. I can introduce you." His words were ground out.

Was he offering other men for me to make out with, to combine my scent with?

Hurt bloomed in my chest.

The bastard *really* didn't want me.

"Let's do it now. You can sleep while I talk to them," I agreed, hiding the hurt behind my angry façade.

I *was* angry, but mostly...

Overwhelmed.

Worried.

Sad.

Fuck, I hated having emotions.

"Fine." He stepped past me, and my eyes were glued to his backside as he made quick work of the rock wall that really *was* the exit of his home. My body was stronger since I'd become a fae, but I still moved slowly as I began climbing up. It was at least fifteen or twenty feet, so... scary as hell.

Priel's hand stretched out as I neared the top.

I wanted to take it, but then again, I also wanted to be naked with him.

In his bed.

While his face was between my thighs.

Yeah, I needed to chill.

To focus, too.

My mind was a mess. Guess that came with the territory of the fae you were crushing on introducing you to his friends so you could hook up with them.

Maybe I'd get lucky and it would end up like one of those reverse harem books. A handful of hot, powerful fae would declare me theirs and be more than happy to dote on me and share me, and I'd never have to look at or dream about Priel again.

Although, I was a virgin. So, not really sure I'd know what to do with one dick, let alone five.

Maybe I should just hope one of them would catch my fancy and fill my dreams from here on out.

I ignored Priel's outstretched hand, hauling myself out of the cave and collapsing on my ass before I took a quick look around. The space was rocky, and there were massive, harsh cliffs surrounding us.

When I looked overhead, I saw a bunch of flying creatures. They had to be fae, but the jagged rocks far above us jutted out in spiked angles, protecting us from the winged beasts.

"Why is she bleeding?" A low male voice jerked my attention to the group of men around us.

I tried not to take a step back when I saw them.

There were so many massive male fae surrounding me, it made my head spin. They were all wickedly strong, but with a variety of skin colors and face shapes. Every one of them was totally inked-up, just like Priel.

I counted them silently.

Nine.

Nine damn men.

Please let this not be a reverse harem situation.

Nine dicks was way, way too many for this chick.

Nope, I could not do it.

Not my thing.

Send help.

"Stuck herself with my tattoo pen," Priel grumbled. "North wants to get to know you while I sleep. Don't overwhelm her, and don't even fucking think about touching her."

With that, the bastard shifted and jumped smoothly back into his cave.

Asshole.

I tried not to let my body fold inward at the thick weight of the fierce attention of eight massive, gorgeous men.

"We'll take turns. Alphabetically," one of the men finally growled.

The others grunted their agreement, and quickly made themselves sparse, leaving me with one of the guys. He had dark skin, and I tried not to stare at the colorful tattoos stretching across his body. They weren't as gorgeous as Priel's, but they were still gorgeous.

"Who does all of your ink?" I asked him, peeling my eyes off him and focusing out on the forest in front of us. "Most of it is in the same style."

I was ninety-nine-percent sure I already knew the answer, but wanted to be certain.

"Priel. Manipulating magic thoroughly enough to mark the skin permanently requires more power than most of us could imagine," the man admitted.

Dammit.

"What's your name?" I checked.

Hopefully someone had set a timer or something. If I was going to speed-date a bunch of fae, I needed that damn timer to keep it from getting awkward.

"Bovay."

"Nice to meet you, Bovay." My words were polite, even though I didn't feel them.

A stretch of silence had me cringing inwardly.

"So, how does the pack work? Priel is the leader?" I asked, trying to keep things from getting worse.

"We have no leader. Priel was branded by Vevol, so he's the strongest of us. We respect him because of that, but we're a family, not a kingdom."

So they didn't do the Alpha shit that werewolves supposedly did according to the many romance books I'd read on Earth.

"What does that mean? That he was *branded by Vevol*?" I asked carefully, making sure not to come across as too eager or curious. Suspicion was not something I wanted to attract.

"Vevol chooses the strongest fae and blesses them with an extra gift of power."

So Priel had told me the truth.

Dammit again.

I searched my mind for another question. There was so much shit I didn't know, and hadn't had a way of finding out. I just had a hard time remembering all of the questions when I was in the moment.

"Why did some of the fae follow me here when they could all just wait back at the Stronghold to meet the other women?" I asked. "Wouldn't that be easier?"

"It's all about scent." Bovay tapped the side of his nose. "The fae are in line to meet the females that smell the best to them. Those are probably their best chance for a compatible mate."

Oh.

I wasn't sure whether that was interesting or insulting.

"So when a guy isn't interested in me, it's because I smell wrong?" I asked.

"Or just don't smell right," Bovay agreed.

Damn.

Maybe that was why Priel had never wanted me.

I *just didn't smell right* to him.

That made me want to punch something, though.

"Why don't you guys smell different to me, then?" I asked.

"You haven't shifted."

Huh.

"Does shifting hurt?" I had always wondered that, but never been brave enough to ask.

"Of course not. You're a hound as much as you're a fae."

I'd never thought about it like that.

"Can you teach me how?" I asked him, suddenly sort of eager. I'd fought so hard not to shift back in the Stronghold, but now...

Well, I wanted to try it. To see what happened.

"After you've met the rest of the pack," Bovay agreed. "You don't smell right to me."

Of course I didn't.

With him, I was kind of glad about that though.

He stood and nodded toward me before strolling off into the trees. Another man came out immediately, jogging over to me and sitting down.

He flashed me a grin, and I fought one of my own. I couldn't help it; the guy was gorgeous, and looking at me like he thought I was too.

"I'm North," I offered.

"I know. I'm Clevv." He offered me a hand, in a very human gesture that he must've learned just for a situation like this one.

Not wanting to be rude, I shook his hand. Most of the time, I didn't mind the rudeness. Rudeness was good for creating space between you and the people you wanted space from.

But it also hurt people, and I felt bad about that often.

"You have beautiful hands," he offered me, as he shook my hand longer than was necessary."

My face heated. "Thanks."

"Are you an artist?"

"How did you know?"

He chuckled. "There's paint beneath your fingernails. I'm surprised Priel's flames didn't burn it away."

Oh.

"His flames didn't feel hot when he was running here."

The man lifted an eyebrow. "That takes a lot of control. I should thank him for taking care of my future mate so well."

A snort escaped me, and he flashed me a grin as I slipped my hand out of his. "So how bad do I smell to you?"

"You smell like smoke curling off a cooking klomre. Fucking delicious."

I bit back another snort. "I'm not looking for a permanent mate. I just need someone to bond with so my scent changes enough that the other guys stay away."

"You can use me in any way you'd like." He winked at me.

A laugh escaped me. "I'll keep that in mind."

"So what kind of things do you paint?" His expression was so full of interest that I couldn't stop myself from answering.

"My dreams, mostly. I have strange, vivid dreams."

He looked intrigued. "Some say Vevol herself communicates through dreams."

"Do they?" I didn't buy into that shit, so I feigned interest. "I've never heard that before. None of the other fae ever referred to your world as a goddess before, either."

"Different types of fae have different beliefs. All of us feel that Vevol is female, and alive. Some believe she has a physical form and can appear to people. Hellhounds, for the most part, believe she is the consciousness of our world as a whole, without a fae-shaped body."

Interesting.

January had never said anything about that, and she knew the fae much better than any of the other girls who had been in the Stronghold.

"What about the dragons?"

"Dragons are solitary fae. They don't run in packs, other than Lian. And he only works with the rest of the Wild Hunt because there has to be one of each type. Though dragons typically believe that Vevol is alive, they have no reason to think she has thoughts or a will of her own."

Huh.

He continued explaining the beliefs of the fae as I went through the different types, and I tried hard to store all of the information for later. I didn't ever have anything to contribute to the other girls in the Stronghold, but maybe if I did...

Well, maybe things could change.

It wasn't likely.

I had pushed them away for a long time. At first, because I was scarred by the way I'd been ripped away from my family. And then, because of my awful dreams.

But there was a chance that I could maybe become friends with them, and honestly, I wanted that. Even though it sounded really out of my reach.

The next fae replaced Clevv after a bit more time had passed, and then a new fae was sitting down next to me.

Time moved quickly. The fae were mostly friendly, though three of them were painfully awkward. I did my best to keep the conversation moving with all of them (despite my own awkwardness), and learned a hell of a lot more about the fae than I had ever known.

.   .   .

THE SUN HAD SET when I finally made it through the last man, and then they all made their way back over and reformed the group they had been in earlier. I chatted with a few of them, appreciating the new, relaxed feel that the group had taken on after I got to know them all a little.

I wasn't ready to choose one of them to be my mate permanently—that much, I was positive about—but I did need to connect myself to another man to free myself from Priel.

And I was really hoping the end of our connection would be the end of my damned sex dreams about him.

When my stomach growled, all of us made our way to a cave nearby where we could eat. It was shaped the same way Priel's place was, with a big drop into it and a climbing-wall leading out. The inside held a large kitchen, though, with a pantry of sorts built into the stone walls and filled to the brim with food.

Across from the kitchen, there were a few massive cushion-things that reminded me of large bean bags. Those of the men who didn't start cooking settled onto them, still talking and laughing. They were discussing a hunt they had done together, so I mostly ignored them.

My mind went back to the hot moment with Priel earlier.

The way he'd had me pinned against the wall, and his body's clear desire for me.

My heart clenched as I remembered his disgust with the idea of having sex with me.

Fuck, I needed to get away from him.

Not just distance-wise, but emotionally.

My gaze slid over the men before it settled on the flirty Clevv, who had joked about me being his future mate.

He felt me staring, and flashed me a grin.

The man had offered to let me use him. He didn't care whether or not I wanted permanence—which I didn't, yet.

He was the perfect choice.

I let the decision to form a temporary bond with him settle in my mind as we all ate together. The food was incredible, and *so* different than what I'd eaten back in the Stronghold. It was nice to try something new, honestly.

And after we were done, I was ready to try something *else* new.

Making out with a fae.

It was go time.

THREE

THE OTHER MEN TRICKLED OUT, some of them headed for their homes to sleep for the night. Others went out to guard the land we were in, though they reassured me that no one was stupid enough to waltz in without assuming they'd lose their head.

But Clevv stayed, and I did too, until we were the only ones left.

Swallowing my nerves, I walked over to the bean bag he was pretending to doze on.

His eyes opened, and he gave me a slow, animalistic grin. "Decided to take me up on my offer?"

I forced myself to bite back a smile. "I did."

He sat up, maneuvering so he was sitting on the edge of the bean bag with his feet pressed against the floor.

I stepped closer, and his hands remained on his knees.

"Here." I grabbed his hands and awkwardly set them on my hips.

A rumble of approval escaped him as his fingers slowly squeezed, feeling my body through my clothes.

No way in hell were those things coming off.

The brands needed to stay hidden, after all.

And honestly, I wasn't super attracted to Clevv. He was gorgeous and had a great smile, and I hoped he could make me forget about my eighteen months of attraction to Priel. But he didn't make my blood hot or turn me on the way the blond hellhound did.

Then again, if *hot blood* was the only reasoning behind why I was with a guy, I'd probably end up regretting that decision at some point.

Maybe not at the beginning, but eventually.

I'd never kissed a guy before my awkward peck with Priel, but after so many insanely-realistic, hot dreams, I didn't hesitate when I pressed my mouth to Clevv's.

He let me take the lead, his hands gentle on my hips while I slid my tongue into his mouth.

He groaned, parting his lips and swiping his tongue against mine. He didn't taste bad, but didn't taste good, either. And his tongue didn't feel wrong... it just didn't feel *right*.

The kissing was still enjoyable though, so I put my hands on his shoulders and stepped a little closer.

He took that as permission to pull me where he wanted me, and dragged my pelvis to his. His erection was near my core, and it felt okay. Not horrible, but not great, just like everything else with him.

I was new to all of it though, so maybe it would get better with time. And none of it felt bad or wrong, so I didn't protest.

His hands dragged up my back, pulling my shirt higher before his fingers dug into my hair.

We kept kissing, and he seemed to be getting hotter and heavier. I wasn't getting horny, but the way his hands moved over my back and in my hair told me he was.

Which meant I probably needed to think about ending the kiss, but I was still mostly enjoying it.

A roar in the distance had me jerking my mouth away from Clevv's, my head turning in the direction of it. We were underground, so I didn't see anything, obviously.

"Someone's always roaring here," he murmured to me. He looked down at my tits, and I noticed that my shirt had ridden up, revealing a strip of skin and two or three of my *brands*. I yanked it down into place as his hands wrapped around my face and dragged my mouth back to his.

I was pretty done with kissing after accidentally flashing him my brands on top of not really feeling it, but let him slide his tongue into my mouth again.

There was a thud off to my left, followed by a furious snarl, and then massive hands were ripping me away from Clevv.

I landed on a squishy beanbag-thing just in time to watch Priel throw the other man against the wall. Priel's fist flew into Clevv's face, and an awful crunch had my eyes widening in horror.

"What the hell?" I sputtered.

Priel's fist slammed into Clevv's face again, and I let out a shocked sound that I didn't want to admit resembled a whimper.

Priel's head jerked toward me, and I saw his eyes flooded with fire. His face was twisted in a furious snarl, and for the first time outside of my insane dreams, there wasn't a shred of humanity in his expression.

The only time he ever looked like that in my dreams was when he was losing himself inside me at the end of a particularly kinky round of sex.

And of course, my body responded to the mental images that flickered in my mind next.

Images of Priel.

Making out with Clevv hadn't done a damn thing to turn me on, but apparently just thinking about the Priel of my dreams was enough to get me going.

Great.

A furious roar escaped Priel, and he slammed another fist into Clevv's face. If Clevv was fighting, I didn't know. I couldn't look at him. Not while I could smell his blood.

My arms wrapped around my stomach, and I hunched in on myself. I wanted to be the kind of chick who ran into a fight and broke it up, but I just... wasn't.

Five more thuds sounded, one after another.

"What happened?" another male hound growled.

"Help me get Priel off of him," another one ordered.

All of them launched into the fight.

My arms squeezed my abdomen painfully tight, and I watched in awful, tense fear as they wrestled Priel away from Clevv. Clevv collapsed to the ground immediately after Priel was removed from him, and I hoped like hell that he wasn't dead.

"North," one of the men wrestling Priel snarled. "Come over here, now."

His command had me freezing in place even more completely.

What if Priel hurt me?

What if—

"He's going to kill us if you don't get over here," another man snarled.

That was enough to get even my terrified ass off the beanbag.

I hurried over to them.

One of them grabbed my arm, rolling away as he yanked me downward. He shoved me right on top of the fighting Priel, his gigantic hands pressing me into the furious hellhound now bucking beneath me.

My long, dark hair hit him in the face, and he froze.

A slow, feral snarl escaped him, and my whole body tensed.

His hands landed roughly on my hips.

They were in exactly the same place Clevv's had been, but the feeling was vastly different. He didn't just touch me because he liked the way I felt—he gripped me possessively, like I belonged to him.

Like he would kill anyone who tried to take me from him.

That had to be in my head. I knew it had to be in my head.

But I still couldn't stop the warmth in my chest because of it.

"We have to get out of here," one of the other men said in a low voice. "Someone grab Clevv."

"North," one of the men said.

Priel snarled furiously, and his needy grip on my hips tightened painfully. I didn't hate the pain, though. It made me feel more alive than I'd felt in the entirety of the eighteen months I'd been in Vevol.

There was a moment of silence, and then the same man said, "He won't hurt you. His beast side has taken over, and reason won't work. But he won't hurt you."

I hadn't thought he would hurt me, but the words still made me feel better.

Still, I tried not to react to them. Priel didn't seem to like the other men talking to me in his current *state*.

I remained where I was as I heard sounds that had to be the other hellhounds climbing out of the cave. My face was on Priel's chest, and I could hear his heart pounding furiously.

Despite his stillness, the man wasn't calm. Not even close.

A few minutes passed, and then he roughly rolled us both. I was pinned below him, his flaming eyes staring down at me while almost every hard inch of him pressed against me.

A long, tense moment passed.

His lips curled up in a snarl, his body heating before he growled fiercely, *"Mine."*

I stared at him with wide eyes.

Fuck.

Maybe Priel-the-man didn't want me, but Priel-the-hound seemed to feel the same way I did.

But since I wasn't sure how much of the moment man-Priel would remember, I didn't reply with the breathy, "yes" that my horny, dream-obsessed self wanted me to.

Instead, I just stared.

And waited.

A few minutes passed, and then the hellhound's nostrils flared as he inhaled deeply.

Another pissed snarl escaped him, and then suddenly he was on his feet, and I was hanging over his shoulder. A yelp escaped me as he flew up the climbing-wall, and I wrapped my arms around his abdomen from behind when he started sprinting toward his cave. I bounced a little, but held onto him for dear life as he ran.

His hands held my hips again as he launched us into the hole that was his cave's entrance, and his hold prevented me from feeling the impact of the landing.

A moment later, we were in the bathroom, and his hands were ripping my shirt over my head.

My mind spun, trying to keep up with the furious man as my long-sleeve top hit the floor. My hair fell to my belly button, wild and tangled, and my chest rose and fell quickly

"What are you doing?" I breathed to the man, when his hands found the bottom hem of the fireproof tank top I wore as a bra.

"*Mine*," he snarled at me.

I tried to stop myself from gawking at the words, but probably failed.

His hand caught a fistful of my hair, and lifted it to his nose. When he inhaled, the fire in his eyes turned bluish white, and he roared.

My stomach clenched.

Shit.

Priel's beast side seemed to have decided that I belonged to him, at least for the moment. Probably because of that little peck that started the mating process for us. If kissing another guy had ended said mating process, there was a decent chance that Priel's illogical mind wanted him to reform the bond or restart the process.

I didn't really want to be bonded to Clevv after the less-than-pleasurable makeout session—especially if Priel had decided he was interested in me after all—so I wasn't against that. My first priority just needed to be calming down Priel, before he actually *did* kill someone.

I was fairly certain he was stripping me because he wanted me in the shower, so I could wash off Clevv's smell. But I was also pretty sure that the mating process came with a smell of its own, which meant I couldn't scrub the other man's scent off entirely.

I could at least clean my hair and body, though.

Priel ripped my fireproof tank over my head without pausing to check out my tits.

Clearly, he wasn't stripping me because he wanted me naked. He just wanted to change my scent. Which was both a relief and an offense at the same time.

His hands were tugging down my pants and the fireproof shorts I wore as underwear a moment later, and I bit my lip when he kneeled in front of me, his face right in front of my core.

How many of my dreams had started that way?

Too many.

Too damn many.

He freed my feet from the clothes, apparently unaffected by my nudity or the many brands on my skin.

My pants were tossed across the bathroom, and then he was hauling me off the ground. I shrieked when he threw my bare body over his shoulder, his massive hands hot on the back of my thighs as he turned on the water.

Another shriek escaped me when the icy stream hit my ass, and I writhed against him, trying to get away from it.

His hands slid up and gripped my ass firmly.

I froze when the warmth of his palms blossomed, heating my skin as the water slowly began to warm too.

My eyes closed, and as much as I tried not to, I enjoyed the hell out of that touch.

When the water was finally hot, and I was enjoying his palms on my backside far too much, he ripped me off his shoulder and set me down on my feet.

Steam filled the air as hot water rolled over my skin. My eyes locked with Priel's burning orbs for a moment until he grabbed another long chunk of my hair and lifted it to his nose.

Another ferocious snarl escaped him.

He spun me around, pushing my chest to the wall of his shower. My tits kissed the stone, my palms lifting to brace myself against it. The scent of something fresh flooded my nose, and then hot hands were scrubbing my scalp and hair.

Those long fingers tilted my head back as he began to rinse the soap from my strands, and my eyes closed.

The man was insane, but honestly, my own feelings and emotions were such a source of whiplash that his demanding tendencies didn't bother me. And truthfully, I thought the moment was blissful. I liked his growliness, and the way he was pulling me around made me feel sort of... desired.

He washed my hair two more times, sniffing the strands between each new round of soap, before he was satisfied that it was free from Clevv's smell.

My whole damn body tensed, my palms pressing hard against the shower wall as his large hands dragged over my back, soaping me up.

Though he didn't linger on any particular part of me (even the sensitive ones), my eyes nearly rolled into the back of my head as his hands slid over my arms, down the curves of my sides, and over my nipples. I inhaled sharply as he palmed my breasts unintentionally, and my body clenched as his hands dragged down to my core.

He cleaned everything.

Everything, everything.

Literally, every fold in my lady parts, every squishy curve of my body, every crack between my toes.

He even grabbed a tube of the fae's strange verson of toothpaste, then slid his fingers into my mouth and scrubbed my tongue.

And it felt incredible.

All of it.

When he inhaled against my back and growled, determining that I still smelled like Clevv, I sent up a prayer of gratitude to Vevol, in case she existed the way Clevv seemed to think she did.

Because then Priel washed me again.

And again.

I was a puddle of horny Jello when he was finally satisfied with the way I smelled. The water shut off, and he palmed my face before he caught me on fire, as if trying to burn away whatever nonexistent pieces of Clevv's touch were still attached to me.

After a few moments, his fire died, and then a thick towel wrapped around me.

When Priel turned me around and lifted me up, the fire still burning in his eyes, my legs wrapped around his hips as he carried me toward his bed.

He lowered me carefully to the mattress before positioning himself over the top of me.

Fuck, he was huge.

I practically drooled at the expanse of bare, art-covered skin and muscle above me.

His flaming eyes devoured my face for a long moment, before he leaned down and kissed me.

I'd already been kissed that day, but the moments with Clevv were downgraded to swapping spit the first moment Priel's mouth took mine.

His hands were hot and rough on my thighs, the length of his cock pressing against my center while his lips, teeth, and tongue devoured mine. He kissed me like I was the air he needed to breathe, and fuck, it was *everything*.

His hands pried my legs open wider, and I cried into his mouth as his massive erection rubbed against me exactly the way I needed it to.

I was coming undone seconds later, keening into his mouth as pleasure rolled through my body, hotter and fiercer than I'd imagined it would feel even in the steamiest of my dreams.

When I came down from the high, I looked around the bed in dazed shock.

I frowned slightly when I didn't see him on the bed.

Slowly, and with a groan, I rolled to my side to see if he'd walked back to the bathroom.

But the door stood wide open, and it was definitely empty.

My stomach clenched as I eased myself to my feet, looking around the entirety of the small home.

Nothing.

He was gone.

The bastard had left me alone in his bed after getting me off without even touching me.

Had he really hated it that much?

Or had he really been that disgusted by me?

Hurt bloomed within my chest, and tears stung my eyes.

Of course this had happened.

When had things ever actually worked in my favor?

I was exhausted, but too furious with the fiery blond bastard to sleep.

So I stormed back to the bathroom to grab my clothes—silently thrilled that they smelled like another man.

I halted in the doorway when I found the floor bare.

After I blinked a few times, dragging my mind back to those minutes when he'd undressed me, I looked behind the door. And behind the toilet. And in the cabinets, for good measure.

They were gone.

The bastard had not only ditched me, but took my clothes with him when he did so.

Fury had me literally shaking as I stomped to the box near his bed, where I'd seen his clothes organized neatly. I dug through the shit in there, unfolding everything in an effort to piss him off when he bothered to return.

I found shorts.

Pants.

More shorts.

And more pants.

That was it.

No tops.

I snarled as I yanked the pants up my legs.

The magic in my belly clenched and pulsed with my fury. It was the fire within me, trying to break free. Attempting to make me shift.

And I wasn't having it.

The only way to stave off the bitchy magic rolling around within me was to drown it out with paint, so I stormed over to Priel's art shelves and grabbed the brushes and paint off of them.

Anger coursed through me as I filled one of his clean, perfect-looking palettes with the colors that spoke to my raging soul.

I was too furious to even bother with covering a wall in black or white to give myself a blank slate.

No one needed a blank slate when they were this pissed.

My fingers and brush moved together as I slapped my emotions onto the wall of Priel's home, immortalizing every shred of anger I could manage.

And when I couldn't keep my eyes open any longer, I collapsed onto his perfectly clean sheets and blankets without rinsing the paint off my skin.

Four

Priel

I STORMED INTO THE FOREST, one fist clenched around North's clothes and the other wrapped around my erection. The clothing caught fire at my will as it fell to the dirt, my spare palm bracing itself against the tree as I pumped my cock. It didn't even take a whole damn stroke before I came undone with a savage roar, the image of my female's naked body painted across my mind in every shade of red there was.

She wasn't mine.

I shouldn't think of her as mine, even when I was half-shifted and operating on instinct.

But...

Fuck, she was mine.

I couldn't handle any alternative.

I'd kept my distance when she'd shown no interest eighteen months earlier. Her scent hadn't demanded every ounce of my attention the way the other males' explained it did when a female was their mate, so I gave the other men time to see if she was theirs. That was my damn obligation.

I had kept my distance until the fact that slow-developing mate bonds were possible was revealed.

And then I'd made sure she'd drawn my name, so I'd be the one fighting for her.

Then she'd kissed me, and clearly been uncomfortable. So when she slammed her door in my face, I let her.

And when she didn't emerge from her room, I took the hint.

But when she'd kissed Clevv, I couldn't fucking take it.

I had warned my pack not to touch her. I had tried to make sure that none of them tested me. They should've known not to risk my fury.

Yet he'd kissed her.

My female.

My *mate.*

And I had fucking lost it.

I'd stripped her.

Cleaned her.

Touched her.

Kissed her, the way I'd wanted to since the moment I caught her scent.

Unraveled her on my cock, without taking her completely.

Now she was going to hate me even more than she already did, and yet I couldn't bring myself to regret it.

Not when she was in my home, her scent intertwined with mine the way it was supposed to be.

Not when her soft, bare skin was wrapped in my sheets, sprawled across my bed.

An image of her naked body filled my mind, and I clenched my cock in my fist again, still infuriatingly hard.

She was absolutely covered in Vevol's brands. There were three on one of her arms, five on the other. A large one stretched across one of her breasts. So many of them dotted her abdomen, one of them stretching in a harsh line that spoke to me in ways I couldn't find words to describe.

They spread down her back in various sizes, over that sexy little ass, down the thighs I wanted to lick every inch of.

I was stroking my cock again, I realized, my chest heaving harshly.

She had taken possession of my mind.

I would make her a part of my soul if it killed me.

To do so, I would need to win her heart. Considering her hatred for me, that wouldn't be an easy task.

The memory of the way her body had arched against mine, her flame-flooded eyes dilating as she'd teetered on the edge of her pleasure, made me roar as I came undone once more.

I'd have her again, completely. I'd mark her in every fucking way there was, before anyone else had the chance to realize how powerful or special she was.

Vevol's connection to her didn't matter. What mattered was that she would smell of me, the way January smelled of Calian.

...As soon as I figured out how to convince her that she was mine.

FIVE
NORTH

I WOKE up to the smell of cooking food, and the sound of running water.

My stomach growled, and I groaned as I struggled to work my sluggish mind through everything that had happened before I crashed.

The kissing—lots of kissing.

The abandonment—shit, I *hated* Priel. Or at least *wanted* to hate him.

The painting—so much painting.

Why was it all so damn overwhelming?

It took me a few minutes to talk myself out of bed.

My feet met the warm stone floor when I finally managed to get myself up.

I looked down at my bare chest at the same time Priel glanced over his shoulder. He was standing in front of the sink, washing something, while food sizzled in a pan a few feet to his right.

Yeah, I didn't have a shirt.

And why the hell was he so gorgeous?

It was stupidly unfair.

I threw an arm over my tits, growling, "Where the hell did you put my clothes?"

"In the box." His eyes lingered on my skin for a long moment before he turned back to whatever he was washing. The food he had cooking smelled incredible, not that I wanted to admit it.

I stomped over to the box, pulling out my fireproof underwear and quickly tugging them on. Priel's admittedly-comfortable pants remained on the ground as I bent over, digging through the smallish box.

Where was my shirt? My pants? I needed those, badly.

"Where did you put my *actual clothes*?" I snapped at the hellhound in the kitchen.

"The shirt and pants? They're ash."

I waited for the apology.

For the promise that he'd get me new shit.

The nonchalant mention that he had a change of clothes for me ready right that minute.

None of those things came.

The bastard even started whistling as he continued washing whatever the hell had his complete attention.

"I can't leave like this," I finally snarled at the man.

"No," he agreed. "You'll have to shift so we can run back to the Stronghold without letting anyone see your brands. The way our scents have intertwined should buy us a few weeks, at least."

"So I have to learn how to shift—something I don't want to do —because *you* couldn't stop yourself from burning *my* clothes?"

"You have to learn how to shift so that you're not consumed by your inner fire," he said bluntly, without turning around. "And I wouldn't have needed to burn your clothes if you hadn't decided to kiss one of my packmates."

"Why would you care? You've never wanted me." I stood up, my fists clenching at my sides as fire throbbed in my abdomen, my magic still desperate to make an appearance.

He finally turned around, and I saw what he'd been scrubbing.

A paintbrush I'd left in a cup of water.

They worked the same after that, but they did stain a bit thanks to the nature of Vevol's version of paint. And the bastard clearly had a problem with stains.

His eyes narrowed at me. "Not *wanting* you and not *claiming* you are two entirely different things. I've wanted you since the first moment I caught your scent."

I scoffed, the magic in my abdomen pulsing so hotly it physically hurt to keep it under control. "Don't lie to me."

His eyes burned for a moment, before the fire faded.

The paintbrush met the counter, and he stalked across the room. I stood my ground, not sure I could control my magic and move at the same time. It was pulsating more intensely than it ever had before, and I was starting to think I might not be able to get it back under control.

His hand pressed to the bare skin on my abdomen, left exposed by my tank top, and my fire pulsed in response. My fists were clenched so tight they hurt.

His voice was low and gentle when he spoke, surprising me with his lack of anger. "Don't do this; don't fight your magic. Holding back your anger or your flames disrupts your energy. Should it break through, it'll force a shift and you'll be trapped in your other form for days, if not weeks."

"January never said that," I told him through gritted teeth.

"January isn't a hound. Dragons and phoenixes have fire; you and I *are* fire."

"Then what do I do?" My voice bordered on desperate.

I'd never felt my magic this close to taking over before.

"Let out a slow breath and unclench." He removed his hand from my abdomen, showing me a fist and then slowly opening it. "Let yourself burn."

"It might force me to shift," I said, panicking a little.

"It might," Priel agreed.

"I don't want to," I hissed.

"Eventually, the fire won't give you a choice." His eyes were serious, and I hated to admit it, but I believed him.

"Can you stop it?"

His eyes darkened. "If you give me your whole name, yes."

Shit.

Whole names had power. If I gave him my whole name—or my actual name, in my case—he could force me to come to him, wherever he was. That was the only thing I really knew about full names, but they had to have more power than that, didn't they?

"No," I shot back.

"Then embrace the shift. I'll diffuse the fire, so it's comfortable for you." His palm landed on my skin again, his fingers stretching over my belly. His flames moved across his hand, and I felt the magic that had tensed in my abdomen begin to slowly unclench.

His fire trailed over me, and my breathing slowed.

My eyes closed.

More relief than I'd realized I needed seeped through me as his magic intertwined with mine and both lazily slid through my veins.

My back arched slightly, and then I felt myself falling.

I caught myself with a thud, and when I forced my eyes open, found myself on all fours.

When I looked down and saw burning paws, my head spun.

Priel's fingers stroked my head slowly, his touch and his flames calming me.

Why did that feel so good?

I looked at him, and his lips curved upward slightly. "Like the others probably told you, hounds are pack animals. Our fire craves fuel, and we fuel each other. My flames showed yours that they were safe."

Oh.

I supposed that made sense. It was probably a better answer than the one I'd assumed, anyway.

But I'd assumed it had something to do with the mate bond we'd started, and Priel didn't even want the bond, so that wouldn't have made sense anyway.

"You might be stuck in this form for a while," he told me, his hand still stroking my head. It felt really good, even if I didn't want to admit that. "Let me finish cooking and cleaning up, and then you can decide whether you want to stay here or head back to the Stronghold. I still need to rest, but I can sleep on the floor of your room if you'd prefer."

Fuck.

I wasn't looking forward to making any of those choices.

He returned back to the kitchen though, making things easier for me for the time being.

I WATCHED him cook and clean.

Not only did he have an incredible ass, but he was good at everything.

He didn't mind the work of scrubbing paint off the brushes. He didn't seem bothered as he studied (for the tenth time) the mural of flames and burning flesh that I'd left on his wall. He even whistled while he cooked.

And when I ate off a plate with my tongue like a damned animal, he grinned proudly and told me that I was one of them now.

A hellhound.

It was surreal.

WHEN THE TIME TO make a decision came, I reluctantly agreed to stay with him for a few days while he caught up on rest. He seemed relieved by the idea, and thanked me before he finished cleaning up my messes, and then went to sleep.

Since there was only the one bed, I reluctantly curled up next to him on it. When I fell asleep in my hellhound form, for the first time in over a year and a half, I slept peacefully.

A WEEK PASSED SIMILARLY.

Priel cooked and cleaned. He fed me, and rubbed my head.

I was starting to feel like his dog—or his mate.

I wasn't sure which option appealed to me more, so I refused to consider either of them.

But I couldn't shift back, which left me with zero alternative options.

Most of the time, honestly, we both slept. I hadn't realized how behind on sleep I was after so many months of nightmares and sex dreams, and the peacefulness that accompanied sleeping in my hound form was addictive.

Almost as addictive as Priel's near-constant grins, jokes, and the feel of his arm draped over my body while we slept.

And his scent?

Now that I'd shifted, I knew exactly what Priel's packmates had been talking about when they said that someone smelled attractive, or right for them.

With nearly every inhale, I was reminded how good the man had tasted. He was like a can of damn Febreeze made just for me, and it was intoxicating.

AFTER THAT WEEK had gone by, Priel looked significantly more relaxed, and I followed him out of the cave. I didn't even have to climb in my hound form; just jumped right the hell out. It was epic.

And the run was incredible.

Priel's pack ran with us. They seemed to have gotten over everything that happened with Clevv, which was a relief.

Priel ran at my side, and the rest of them circled us like they were protecting me. Clevv was kept as far from me as possible

—which Priel made sure of every time he shot a glare over his shoulder.

It was a long, long run, but I honestly had the time of my life.

WHEN WE REACHED the Stronghold and the masses of fighting fae around it, I howled a sad goodbye to the rest of the pack, and they howled back to me. I noticed Priel still eyeing Clevv, but ignored him.

The hot blond wasn't really into me, after all.

The group of gathered fae only came close until they caught a whiff of my changing scent. Then, a whole bunch of them started breaking off, leaving.

Maybe those were the ones who had thought my smell was the most appealing.

Priel shifted and knocked on the Stronghold's door when we were in the clear, none of the fighting fae charging toward us and none of his pack within sight. Mare pulled it open a few minutes later, and frowned when she looked between me and Priel.

"Is that..." she began.

"It's North." His fingers stroked the fur on my head, and I tried to force myself not to nuzzle up against his side. It was more difficult than I would've liked.

"Come in, hurry." She gestured us inside, then hastily closed the door without looking at any of the fighting fae. "What happened? Why didn't they attack you?"

He smirked. "North decided to spend a little more time with me so our scents would merge."

Her eyes widened, and she looked down at me.

I scowled, and Mare took a quick step back.

"She won't hurt you. She's just tired and hungry. I'll be out to make her something to eat soon." He eased me toward the door to my bedroom while my mind reeled.

When he'd shut and locked the door behind us, trapping me in my room with him, his eyes fixated on the nearest wall. I growled at him as he studied one of the more gruesome paintings, wearing a wicked grin.

"Has Vevol been speaking to you, Gorgeous?" he mused.

I snapped my teeth at him for his use of the awful nickname he'd taken to calling me, earning a chuckle.

Damn him.

I snapped my teeth again and he held his arm out for me, his grin widening. "Go ahead. All yours."

I withdrew quickly, and he snorted.

His attention moved back to my paintings, and I growled at him again even though it hadn't done a damn thing thus far.

"I like your style," he told me, his hand sliding into the fur on top of my head. "It's much more fluid than mine, and it suits you."

If I'd been in human form, I would've blushed.

It was probably the best compliment I'd ever received.

No one ever really saw my art on Earth, and that hadn't changed since I came to Vevol. Priel's experience was the opposite; his entire pack wore his art proudly, and the man himself was a walking advertisement.

He stepped up closer to the wall with the most gruesome painting, studying it more carefully. Not wanting to see his reactions, I huffed and walked over to my bed, collapsing on the mattress. When it suddenly caught fire, I yelped, jumping off of it and lunging away.

Priel put out the flames with a simple hand motion, and then gestured for me to go over to him. Ignoring the smell of burnt bedding, I reluctantly padded to his side.

"Vevol has been sending you warnings," he told me, his voice no longer playful. "I recognize all of the fae in this painting. That's no coincidence. And given the many brands she left on your skin, Vevol has clearly chosen you as a vehicle for her warnings."

I scoffed.

He stroked my fur, and my body unconsciously moved closer to his.

The man hadn't noticed the small details from my dreams of the two of us that had embedded themselves in my paintings yet, thankfully. Mostly, they were just small, hidden images of his tattoos. I hoped he *wouldn't* notice them. My mind tried to push me to illustrate the scenes in detail, but I'd managed to prevent myself from doing so. If I painted a large image of Priel making love to me, there wasn't a damn chance I would ever move past my obsession with him.

"You see fae burning," he murmured, walking over to another wall. "Hounds, even."

I didn't bother nodding.

The walls were proof enough of what I'd seen.

"Do the other women know?" He looked down at me.

I shook my head in a "no".

"Hmm." He moved to the next wall, which my bed rested against. It was a simple mattress with a large headboard. I'd pushed it forward enough to paint behind it ages ago, and never pushed it back, but it hid the shit I'd painted there anyway.

I *much* preferred that he didn't see that painting, but fought the urge to cover it with my body.

He studied the image silently before moving to the fourth. Relief coursed through me. He hadn't noticed the brief bits and pieces of his tattoos embedded in the other paintings, which was a huge relief.

As long as he didn't look behind the bed, I was in the clear.

He finally walked me into the bathroom, quiet and contemplative. When he stepped into the shower, I growled at him.

His lips curved upward in amusement. "I'm not going to make you shower, Gorgeous. I was going to catch myself on fire to clean my skin. It's more effective than water, even if you don't *feel* quite as refreshed as if you took a real shower."

Oh.

I took a step back, giving him permission. He had a point about the flames; after being constantly on fire over the last week and a day or two, I felt clean, despite running through the forest for so long.

His body was engulfed in flames for a long moment, before the fire died. Then, the man crossed the bathroom again. He looked clean and fresh, and his white-blond hair was even spiked up all pretty-like.

He was hot as hell.

Why he was the one calling me *Gorgeous*, I didn't know. It didn't feel like he was mocking me, though. At least not completely. Maybe that was why it pissed me off so much though; because I didn't believe he meant it completely when he called me that.

"I'm going to make you something to eat," he told me, stroking my head again. "Do you want to stay in here or cook with me?"

I scowled at him, pointing toward the bed with my nose. It was still smoking slightly.

"We'll bring some jilui petals back next time we leave; they're the easiest to find of the plants that make our homes fireproof." He scratched me behind my ears lightly.

I shook off his hand, earning a chuckle as I stalked into the middle of the room, where I wouldn't put anything in danger.

He left the space without a backward glance at me, and I collapsed on the tile with a huff.

Why did I have to be so damn attracted to him? Why couldn't I just let it go? The more time I spent with him, the more I was going to want the bastard, and the last thing I needed was to want him more. My dreams were bad enough already.

Though I considered grabbing some paint and covering the bits and pieces of the paintings that could clue Priel in to my dreams about him, I shot the idea down.

All that would do was make him curious, and something told me I wasn't going to be able to hide the truth from him if he really decided he was going to figure it out.

I shut my tired eyes, and after a while, managed to fall asleep. Shortly afterward, I woke up to eat, and then went back to bed.

Thankfully, since I was still in my hound form, I didn't dream.

WHEN I WOKE UP, my slightly-disoriented gaze caught on Priel. He was sprawled out on the floor beside me, his massive form looking way too at-ease in my space. I stared at him for much longer than I probably should've, struck by the image before me.

He was gorgeous.

So ridiculously gorgeous.

I really needed to move past this obsession.

But how was I supposed to move past something I had dreamed about so many times?

Especially now that he'd kissed me the way he had, and touched me, and...

Shit.

I was screwed.

The urge to paint hit me hard, but I needed hands. My body would need to change. The desire to do so was strong enough to take my breath away, and then suddenly, my body sort of stretched.

I felt myself shifting forms, and relief rolled through me when my bare face met the warm tile I'd been sleeping against. My fireproof tank and shorts were still on, so I wasn't naked.

Easing myself to a seated position, I studied the man on the floor beside me for a few more minutes.

Having him in there with me was seriously messing with my sanity. The whole room would smell like him when he left, and I'd have to figure out a way to clean it, and—

Shit, I needed to get out of there.

I stood up swiftly and crossed the room, carefully opening the door and slipping out.

Mare was sitting on the couch, and she flashed me a quick smile.

My body clenched.

Shit, I couldn't do this.

I couldn't be obsessed with a guy who wasn't really interested in me, who kept calling me Gorgeous, who had snuggled up with me on the floor even though there was a bed just a few feet away.

I was overthinking everything, like I always did.

I didn't know how to talk to him, or be me around him.

I didn't even know what I really wanted from him. Or with him. Or... anything?

Fuck.

I needed fresh air.

Yeah; maybe fresh air could fix things. Or at least help me process somewhat normally.

Turning, I practically ran for the door out of the Stronghold.

My heart pounded rapidly, my body screaming for me to get out.

To move.

To escape.

To *run.*

The only time I'd felt that much stress pointed solely at getting away was when I'd been in that car with my arranged fiancé, and had found out that I was heading toward my death.

The memories melded with my thoughts, tangling in my mind and making me feel like the world was closing in on me. My fingers struggled with the only two locks on the heavy door that someone had bothered doing up, and then I flung the thing open and.rushed outside.

Vevol's humidity met my cheeks, but it wasn't uncomfortable. I hadn't minded the warmth since the fae world had made me one of them.

There were still men fighting outside, but all of the ones who had been looking for me had left when I showed up half-mated to Priel the day before.

We hadn't exchanged vows or had sex, both of which I was fairly certain were the next possible steps in the relationship, but had gotten close enough to doing so to scare the others away or at least discourage them.

I shut my eyes, breathing the fresh air in deeply. It relaxed my shoulders more than I actually expected it to.

There wasn't any fire pulsing in my abdomen anymore, threatening to burn me alive, I realized. Now, the power was just calm and warm and quiet.

That was nice.

A soft breeze caught in my hair. It was smooth and soft, surprisingly enough, and the dark strands blew against my cheek.

Despite the sounds of the fighting, Vevol was a peaceful place. The magic there was—

A hand slid over my cheek.

My eyes flew open, my lips twisting in a snarl as I prepared to rip Priel a new asshole for touching me so suddenly.

The words died in my throat when I found a complete stranger in front of me.

I stepped backward, and collided with a hard chest.

Something screamed within me that it didn't belong to my hellhound either.

Fire erupted on my skin, and I tried to keep my breathing even as I looked around me.

They were everywhere.

Men, encircling me.

Fae with intense eyes, touching me. Not intimately, but still touching me.

"Back off," I finally breathed, struggling the panic that had swelled in my chest.

Confrontation—I was not good with it. Not at all. Sure, I could snarl and growl with the best of them when I felt safe or even safeish, but when I was clearly outgunned?

Panic.

Lots of panic.

I pushed the guy's palm away from my face with a shaky hand, but his lips only curved upward with interest as he withdrew it.

Fucking hell.

What was I supposed to do?

"Vevol has chosen a female," the man who had touched my face mused. "Clevv was right."

Clevv?

Had that bastard noticed my brands while we were kissing?

Had he told someone about—

One of my markings caught my eye, and I froze.

Fuck.

My body stilled when I realized what had just happened.

I had gone outside, into the middle of the fighting.

With my many brands exposed.

Priel had told me they would put me in danger, but that hadn't crossed my mind when I woke up and started panicking.

And now?

Well, I was fucked.

Hopefully not literally.

Unless the blond hellhound bastard was involved, because—

Shit, I needed to stop thinking about him.

What the hell was wrong with me?

I forced my terrified, scattered mind to focus.

There had to be a way to get all of the men to back off long enough for me to get away.

But if the brands really marked me as more powerful than the other women, or something along those lines, then I didn't know if that was even possible.

The sound of flapping wings distracted me, and then a massive phoenix was spiraling down toward me.

Six

I BIT BACK a shriek and tried to move away, but only ended up pressed even harder against the random fae dude still at my back. The one who'd touched my face hadn't come any closer, at least.

The phoenix shifted as he landed, and a small amount of relief cut through me when I realized that I recognized him. He was gigantic of course, with buzzed dark hair and deep brown skin. Thick tattoos wrapped around his biceps, and I recognized the style as Priel's immediately.

This was Ervo.

The Wild Hunt guy who had formed a temporary mating bond with Mare.

He was really damn intense, but quiet. From what I'd seen, he seemed more reasonable to me than some of the other men did.

Especially Priel.

Unhappy murmurs and growls rolled through the group surrounding me.

I tried to step away from the guy who my back was pressed against, but his hands grabbed my arms, and I froze again.

Smooth as a damn snake, Ervo had the man by the throat. My arms were released, and no one else grabbed me.

I watched in horrified fascination as the phoenix's fingers shifted to talons and removed the fae's head from his body before anyone had time to blink.

My eyes widened and my stomach rolled when the head hit the ground with an awful thud.

The phoenix dropped the man's body too, and then his brutal gaze swept the group around me.

Many of the men took a step back.

They were all dangerous, all of the fae, but there was something stronger and deadlier about the Wild Hunt guys.

My eyes were glued to Ervo's hand, my knees knocking together as I watched the blood drip slowly off of his fingertips.

The phoenix's voice was low and deadly as he said, "Fighting over females is understandable. Touching one without her permission is a death sentence."

His gaze dipped to me, but it took me a minute to peel my eyes off of his dripping fingertips.

"Did any others touch you?" Ervo's voice was so calm it was terrifying.

My magic bloomed over my skin, soft flames sliding up my arms as the magic attempted to calm me.

Instinct told me to say no and protect the men who had touched me earlier, just so I didn't have to watch Ervo kill anyone else.

But if I lied about that, what else would the massive group of men expect me to say? Would they think they could grab me, or kiss me, and I'd protect them?

Though nausea settled into my damn bones at the idea of what I was doing, I lifted a finger and pointed across the group, to the man who had touched my face, and then moved my finger to two other men I had seen touch me.

"There were others, too. I couldn't see all of them," I said, fighting to stop my voice from shaking.

All attention settled on the men I'd pointed to, and guilt had my magic weaving and bobbing over my skin.

The three fae sank to their knees, bowing their heads toward Ervo.

Or maybe toward me.

"I was taken by her magic," one of the men said quickly, his voice low and gravelly.

He was so full of it, but I didn't say that aloud.

"Any others who touched her, on your knees." Ervo's voice was still so damn calm.

More fae kneeled around me.

I refused to make eye contact with them, my gaze remaining fixed on Ervo.

"Should any of the females see your faces in the next year, your lives will be forfeit." Ervo's threat wasn't growled or snarled; his calm voice was plenty terrifying. "Should you ever touch a female without her permission again, you will suffer at the hands of your brothers for months before death claims you."

The men shifted forms smoothly. The one nearest to me turned into a massive snake, and out of the corner of my eye, I watched as he slithered away.

I fought a shudder, glad for once that I was a hellhound.

Basilisks were freaky as hell.

"Priel has been hiding her away," a male voice called from somewhere in the crowd. "All of us deserve a chance to show our strength to the female Vevol's chosen. Her power is too great for him to claim her so easily."

Ervo's expression was neutral, but his jaw was clenched slightly. "I don't disagree, but North will decide what she will allow. My female and I will speak with her and determine the best way to approach the situation for all of us. Until then, the fighting ceases."

His gaze swept the group.

Growls and grunts of complaint followed, but grudging nods did as well.

"The hound stays out here with us, though," another one of the men argued.

Ervo dipped his head in agreement, then gestured me toward the Stronghold. I didn't wait for an invitation to go, and the crowd made a path for me as I walked.

When the door was shut behind us, a relieved breath escaped me.

"Where is Priel?" The phoenix asked me calmly.

I pointed toward my bedroom, and he walked in without a pause.

Grunts and growls followed. After Ervo's calm voice spoke—I couldn't make out exactly what he had said—there was a furious snarl.

A disheveled Priel stormed out of the bedroom, and my body tensed as he reached me.

"Where did they touch you?" He stalked around me, lifting my shirt and leaning in to check out my neck.

Oh.

That's what he was looking for? Some kind of evidence that I'd been hurt?

"I'm fine." I pushed his hands away, trying not to let him see how frustrated I was that his reaction was only protective.

Where was the possessive, demanding beast I'd had back in his cave? That was the version of him I wanted; the one that called me *"mine"* and didn't hesitate to claim me in every way.

Or *almost* every way.

"They'll break the door down if you don't join them outside."
Ervo's voice was still infuriatingly calm.

Priel snarled at him.

"She's not going to be safe if they break in here. They've all seen
the brands; there's no turning back now," the phoenix added.

"Fuck." Priel stepped away from me, starting to pace the short
hallway before the door.

"What do they want?" Mare's voice was quiet.

"Me," I said flatly.

"North is covered in Vevol's brands. One brand is evidence that
a fae has been given an extra portion of magic; this many are a
sure sign that Vevol has chosen her for something great," Ervo
explained.

"Damn." Mare's voice was surprised.

"So why can't she just bang Priel to make the bond
permanent?" Sunny checked.

My attention jerked to the other woman. She and Dots were off
behind Mare, watching the interactions but not joining the
argument. I hadn't even noticed them there.

"An hour ago, she could have. Now that they know the truth,
to seal a bond could start a civil war. The best route would be
to come up with a way to establish Priel as the strongest of the
fae who want her," Ervo said.

"How?" Dots asked.

Ervo's and Priel's eyes met before the hellhound growled, "Not a fucking chance."

"It's the simplest way, and our best chance at keeping the peace."

"Do you intend on competing?" Priel snarled back. "Does Nev? Or Teris? Or any of the other bastards who claim to be loyal to us?"

"Are we supposed to know what they're talking about?" Dots whispered to Sunny.

"I don't think so," Sunny grumbled back.

"Slow down and explain," Mare told the men.

A loud, rattling knock shook the whole damn Stronghold. My fire tingled over my skin as the lingering panic from earlier ignited within me.

"You have to leave. This is the only way to keep the peace." Ervo's gaze met Priel's again.

Priel's rough, furious gaze moved to me and lingered. A moment later, he was storming toward the door.

He snarled at the men outside as he opened it, and the damn thing shook our home again when he slammed it shut.

"I am so confused," Dots whispered.

"Join the gang," Sunny muttered back.

"Just start over," Mare told Ervo.

He looked at her, his neutral gaze lingering a bit longer than I would've expected before he looked at me. "When Priel discovered how to work the portal, our fae were restless. The fighting over who would go to your Earth to find the female who called us during the Winter Solstice was fierce, and no decisions were made. Priel finally devised a way to determine who would make up the group who went through; a competition of strength."

He went on, "Each fae competed amongst his own kind, and one of each species was declared the strongest and chosen to participate in the Wild Hunt. The five of us you know were the winners. If you run the same competition and agree to mate with one of the winners, it will focus the other fae and end the fighting temporarily."

Was he serious?

I stared at him for longer than was probably appropriate.

Shit, he really was.

That was their answer for this problem?

A competition?

What the hell were they smoking?

"What happens during the contest?" Mare asked, as I opened my mouth to shoot the idea down.

"It tests the aspects of strength. There's a physical fighting competition, followed by a speed test. The mental dexterity test follows speed, and then the magic test is the final challenge, unless there's a tie. In that case, another physical fight follows."

"That sounds way too complicated," Mare protested.

"It separates the men who are truly interested and worth your time from the ones who aren't," Ervo corrected.

"Not being powerful doesn't make someone not worth our time," Mare argued.

"We could make up our own version of the contest," Dots offered. "One that isn't violent. We could have a bake-off, and a poetry contest..."

I snorted.

The other girls grinned wickedly.

"If you want to put a bunch of men in their places, you'll need to add some kind of sewing competition to that," Sunny added viciously.

Oh hell, it was awful.

But also... kind of awesome.

"Maybe a cleaning contest, too?" Mare teased.

"And a painting one, if we want to touch on North's favorite things," Sunny added. "And give the hellhound bastard a better shot at winning."

"So why are all the fae after you, anyway?" Dots wondered. "I feel like me and Sunny missed something."

I sighed, and gestured to one of the marks on my abdomen. "My burn-bruise things are apparently not considered burns or bruises. The fae call them Vevol's Brands. Only two of the fae guys have them; Priel, and the unseelie king. I guess they're a sign that the person holds unique magic of some sort. Priel's lets him open the portal between our worlds."

The girls' eyebrows were all raised by the time I finished speaking.

"Damn. So you have special magic?" Sunny checked.

"According to them."

"What is it, though?" Dots asked.

I shrugged. "Not a damn clue."

"Well, hopefully a cheesy competition keeps them off our asses for a bit so we can all get outside for a while. I'm tired of being cooped up," Sunny said.

Everyone else murmured agreements.

"I don't know." I grimaced. "I don't want to give them any kind of hope, and then take it away. The way they touched me..." I shook my head. "What if I just tell them that they could write letters or something? That I'll read their letters, and decide if I want to meet any of them?"

"I don't think that will delay them for long," Ervo warned.

"Well, I'm not about to walk out there and tell them that I'm looking to hook up with one of them," I said defensively.

"What if you try to make them stop wanting you, then?" Sunny suggested.

I frowned at her.

She explained her idea. "What if you go out there and tell them that you're in love with Priel? Make up some BS about how you've wanted him since you guys met but you didn't think he was interested? Admit that our matings with the Wild Hunt guys are fake, but you finally admitted your feelings to Priel and he wants you too?"

She continued, "You could tell them that you came back here to grab your stuff so you can retreat back to his love shack and hook up with him in private. The guys are possessive assholes, but it doesn't seem like they want an unwilling woman. If you can make them think that's what you'd be, it might fix this shit."

Her idea was way, way too close to reality for my taste, but what other options were there? As far as ideas went, it was better than my letter one.

I looked at Ervo.

All of us women did, actually.

He grimaced. "It might work... but it also might backfire for the rest of you."

My stomach clenched.

I still didn't know what Priel wanted, and I didn't want to ruin things for the other women.

"We can deal with it for North's sake," Sunny said with a shrug.

Mare and Dots nodded their agreement.

Emotions I didn't want to deal with swelled within me.

They felt a hell of a lot like love. I'd tried hard not to get attached to the girls, and not to let them get attached to me, but maybe it had started happening anyway.

But Priel...

He'd called me his when he was all beastly, and he had acted possessive, but that didn't really mean anything. The fae liked fighting, and he'd never given me a reason to believe that he was really that into me.

I supposed I could always make up some shit about things not working out between us after all of this was over if he wasn't interested in me.

"Well, it's worth a try," I finally, reluctantly said.

Ervo dipped his head in a nod, then strode out of the Stronghold without so much as a glance at Mare.

When I looked over at her, her lips were pressed together in a grimace.

She hid the emotions quickly, looping her arm through Sunny's.

Dots looped hers through mine, and then we started for the door.

"Do you seriously think this is going to work?" I asked them, my voice lowering as we opened the door.

"Depends on your goal. If you want a way to hook up with Priel, definitely." Dots said cheerfully.

I tried not to grimace.

What *did* I want?

That, I didn't know.

"It's show time, ladies. Try not to look interesting," Sunny muttered to all of us as we stepped outside.

The men were all waiting in a massive group, with Priel and Ervo at the front. My eyes went immediately to the massive hellhound, and wow, he looked pissed.

Everyone was silent when myself and the other three girls stepped into a line. Our arms were still linked, I realized.

"The other women and I have been talking," I announced to the men.

My voice carried more than it should've, but I didn't let myself overthink that when there was so much other shit to worry about.

The world was deathly silent around us as the fae waited for me to continue.

"Though it may not be fair to the rest of you, I'm in love with Priel. I have been, since the first day I stepped foot in Vevol. I thought he wasn't interested in me, so I stayed quiet about it, until the other women and I came up with the idea to establish fake mate bonds with the Wild Hunt guys, to protect us from all of you."

The silence seemed to swell around me, so I hurried onward. I wasn't exactly eloquent, but I was pretty sure brutal honesty would get the point across.

"Considering I was attacked when I stepped outside earlier, it's pretty apparent that the protection was necessary," I added.

Priel started to take a step toward me, but Ervo set a hand on his shoulder, holding him firmly in place.

I went on. "Our relationship used to be fake, but when I was in Priel's cave with him, it became real for both of us. We only came back here so I can grab the rest of my things and then go back to his home to be together in peace. I understand that my brands make it seem like I have more power than some of you, and I can assure you that if anyone tries to stop me from mating with the man that I love, I will figure out how to use every drop of that power to end them. This is my life."

I continued, "The person I mate with will be my choice. End of the discussion. You can all talk amongst yourselves and fight about that if you want, but you don't get to mess with us women, regardless of how much power we do or don't possess. Bring your cake or write your letters; we're not just potential mates. We're people, too."

With that, we shuffled back into the Stronghold. I was at the back of the group, and just before I stepped inside, a shadow loomed over me.

Goosebumps went up my arms at the heat rippling off the figure behind me, and I halted.

Priel leaned in until his body was only a breath away from mine. His low growl in my ear was soft enough that no one else could've heard a damn word. "I'm going to be fighting these bastards for a while. My full name is Lopriel. When you're ready, use it."

A shiver rolled down my spine as he stepped away, and I realized the other men were already growling, snarling, and snapping.

My monologue had apparently not done much good. But it had to be better than a competition, I hoped.

As Priel strode toward the other guys, his fists caught fire.

I always tried not to watch him fight, but I'd seen it a few times. And that was exactly how he always started; with the flaming fists.

Fear clenched my stomach.

There were so many other fae. If enough of them got together, they would take him down. He was strong, and he didn't think they would kill him because of the portal he could create, but I didn't trust them.

Not for a second.

I took two steps toward the group, and their attention lifted back to me. I raised my voice louder than I had earlier.

"No more blood. If any more of you bleed today, all four of us will go to the unseelie and mate with the first bastards we find."

My gaze met Priel's, and his eyes were so furious. I could see the fire of his anger burning within them, and knew he was going to be pissed with me.

He *wanted* to fight. And I wasn't on board with it.

He didn't have to love me, or want me, or even like me.

But I wasn't going to let him get himself killed because of me.

Spinning around, I stalked back into the Stronghold. The door slammed behind me, and my fingers shook a little as I did up the top two locks. After a short moment of hesitation, I did the next two too, just to be safe.

"Damn, that was badass," Sunny exclaimed, high-fiving Dots and then Mare. When she held her palm out toward me, it took me a minute, but I finally high-fived her too.

"January is going to be so pissed she didn't see any of that," Mare said, fighting a smile. "Especially that last part. Whew." She fanned herself, and I bit back a grin.

My face ended up forming a terrible grimace, but it was what it was.

"Are you and Priel actually a thing? There was some seriously-steamy eye-banging going on between you two," Sunny said. "If I were you, I'd totally hit that."

I flushed a little. "No. He's never been into me like that. When his eyes shift, he gets sort of possessive, but otherwise he's not interested."

All three girls gave me incredulous expressions.

I bit my lip, taking a step back toward my room.

"Wait a second." Sunny held up a finger. "You seriously think that man—that gorgeous, inked up blond sex god—isn't interested in you romantically?"

"He never acted like it. Things were a little different, back at his house, but only when his mind was shifted. Then he got all caveman, but... no, I don't think he's into me. He just gets possessive because of the bond when someone pushes him." I was rambling, and I knew it. But the alternative was actually letting myself consider the impossible, so... rambling it was.

"North, every man in this world wants a mate. Priel turned Sunny down ages ago, and looked absolutely thrilled when he ended up paired with you after we drew names." Dots gestured to the couches, where he'd been sitting all those months ago.

Shit, I did not need the reminder of that day.

My mind jerked back to the moment he'd stopped me just outside the door, as I was walking in.

I blurted out a question about it without letting myself think it through. "He told me his name when I walked in here. His whole name. What does that mean?"

All three of them stared at me with wide eyes.

"I think Ana would say you're dead," Mare murmured.

"Or start planning your funeral," Sunny tossed out.

Snorts escaped me, and Dots grinned.

Good old Ana.

Honestly, it was nice to remember her, but I was glad she had joined the unseelie. Things had been much happier since then, even for me, and I typically stayed away from everyone else to keep them free from my foul mood.

"Realistically, if I had to guess, I'd say it means he thinks of himself as yours," Mare admitted. "Giving someone your full name is handing them power over you—and that's not something any of the fae would give lightly, even when trying to convince one of us to be his mate. Why did he give it to you?"

"He told me to use it."

Sunny whistled. "He wants you to call him into your room so he can have his dirty, dirty way with you."

My cheeks flushed. "Seriously, Sunny?"

Dots smiled. "Seriously, he probably wants to make sure you're okay. When Ervo woke him up, he was kind of hit with everything at once. And Ervo had some bastard's blood on his hand, so obviously someone did something to you that he shouldn't have. Priel clearly cares a lot about you."

"Clearly to you, but not to me," I muttered.

Her smile morphed into a grin. "That's what friends are for, girly."

My fire rippled over my skin, and I nodded. "Thanks. I'll think about everything you said."

"We're watching a chick flick after dinner, feel free to join us," Sunny called after me. "Also, January will probably break into your room to hear the story when she gets here, so prepare yourself."

I bit back a grin as I shut the door to my room behind me. January wouldn't break in; she valued her own privacy too much to violate mine. But she *would* be pissed that she'd missed the drama.

SEVEN

I WANTED to clear my mind, so I headed into the shower. Before I turned the water on, though, I remembered what Priel had done the last time he was in there. He'd just caught himself on fire, and when the flames died down, he'd been clean.

That sounded pretty nice, so I shut my eyes and reached for the hot magic in my abdomen.

It slid through my body and over my skin, and a warm peace settled some invisible part of me.

I was going to be alright.

When the flames slid back inside me, I let out a long breath.

Honestly, I felt really refreshed.

My fireproof tank and shorts were clean too, so that was nice. Not having to wash them all the damn time would be awesome.

But with that taken care of, I no longer had an excuse not to use Priel's name the way he'd asked me to. If Mare was right, and he really *was* worried about me, I wanted to know.

Plus, I was kind of paranoid that in his anger, he would start a fight, and I would really have to enforce the ridiculous threat I'd made about that.

Which would screw me, basically, because I still wanted the blond bastard.

I made it to the center of my room and wrapped my arms around my abdomen so they didn't fidget awkwardly.

My lips formed the syllables of his name slowly.

Lo—preel

What would happen if I used it? Would he just... appear?

Only one way to find out, I guessed.

Closing my eyes, I let out a slow breath and mentally urged him to come to me with a soft whisper of, "Lopriel."

The air around me burned for a moment, and then there was a massive man in front of me. His eyes were dark, his fire burning in them.

Goosebumps broke out on my arms when his flaming eyes collided with mine.

He usually did my favorite things when his eyes burned like that.

The touching, the kissing...

He stalked toward me, and I took a step backward for every one he took forward until my shoulders met the wall.

His eyes burned me to the damned soul, and I couldn't have looked away if I tried as he continued covering the distance between us.

His voice was low and feral when he asked, "Why did you walk out of the Stronghold without me?"

"I needed air," I whispered.

It wasn't a lie.

"From what?" His low voice gave me more goosebumps.

"You."

He growled furiously in response. "You've exposed your magic to every bastard in my world. Even now, the word is being spread throughout all of the seelies. Soon, the unseelies will learn too, and any number of them could try to take you from me."

"Take me from you? I don't belong to you. We're not mates. You don't even want me."

He snarled at me, his hands pressing into the wall on either side of my head, trapping me in. "You are *mine*, Gorgeous."

I growled back, "You only say things like that when your eyes are glowing. I don't understand why you get possessive and touchy when your eyes glow, and then don't give a damn when they don't. You're giving me whiplash."

The fire vanished from his eyes, but he was still just as furious as he had been a moment earlier.

I froze, not knowing he could change them just like that.

"The world looks slightly different when my mind has shifted, but I can assure you I am just as possessive when my eyes aren't glowing. I told you, I've wanted you since the first time I caught your scent."

I scoffed. "You only stopped by with supplies twice. Don't lie to me."

"A bond didn't snap between us immediately the way it did for January and Lian. I had to give the others time to catch your scent, as was our people's agreement. When I came to see you a third time, after the others had a chance to see if a bond formed, you refused to see me. You weren't interested."

"I refused to see pretty much anyone," I shot back. "Just get out." I tossed a hand toward the door.

"No." He stepped closer to me, and the fronts of our bodies pressed together. The fire in his eyes relit with the contact. "I need to see your skin. To make sure no one hurt you."

"I'm a fae, Priel. Even if someone did hurt me, the evidence would already be gone."

"*Lopriel.*" He all but snarled the word at me. "To you, I am *Lopriel.*"

"You can't have everything you want," I snapped back. "And you *don't* get to choose what I call you."

I was enjoying our argument too much—it was making me all hot and bothered. But he didn't know that, and I couldn't let him walk all over me, or he would think he could just growl and snarl and get his way every time.

"Fine. Call me what you want, but take your damn clothes off. I need to know you're okay." His harsh voice—and choice out of those two options—surprised me.

When his hands tugged my shorts down a heartbeat later, my body flushed.

His hands dragged over my thighs and ass, checking for wounds that didn't exist. When he was satisfied that I hadn't been hurt there, he slid my shorts back up, settling the hem near my waist again. His palms moved over my abdomen, and then tugged the tank top over my head before tossing it to the ground.

"Damn." His eyes burned as they slid over my bare chest, lingering on my tits.

I wasn't injured. His response was solely to the way I looked—which made me feel plenty of dirty things that I couldn't say aloud.

His hands landed on my waist, and he turned me around so my back was to him.

A strangled noise escaped him as they slid down the curves of my hips, stopping there.

I fought a groan.

Would the bastard just grab me already?

Why wouldn't he just touch me the way I wanted him to?

It seemed like he wanted it too, now, so why was he holding back?

"See?" I told him, stepping away from him after a long moment proved he wasn't going to act on whatever he was feeling.

Bending over, I grabbed my shirt off the floor.

"You can go now." I gestured toward the door as I straightened, and tried not to notice that his hot eyes were back on my tits.

"No." His gaze lifted back to mine.

I yanked my shirt over my head, shoving it into place. "What's your excuse this time?"

"We need to figure out what your magic is and how you can use it to protect yourself. The unseelie *will* come when they hear about your brands; you need to be ready for that."

My stomach twisted. "I'm not a fighter. If they come for me, I won't kill them. I don't want those memories hanging over me for the rest of my life."

"I don't expect you to. But I'm hoping your power will give them enough pause to let *me* kill them. We have to be mated by then so that your scent and appearance don't cause a damn war."

I bristled and flushed. Every time I started to think the bastard might be into me, he said shit like that. "I'm not that unattractive. My brands are weird, but they're not *ugly*."

His expression morphed into one of incredulousness. "The way you look and smell will lead them to want you as their *mate*, North. I sure as hell never said you weren't attractive."

Oh.

If he thought I was attractive...

It was time to test him. And his possibly-nonexistent feelings for me.

"Well, maybe I should've done the stupid competition Ervo wanted, then. I'd have the chance to choose some guy, to get out of your hair."

Fury crossed his face.

He started stepping toward me again—doing that thing where he drove me to the wall, and nearly pinned me to the damn thing.

His chest was heaving when my back met said wall. I was breathing fast too.

"You will not be choosing *some guy*. You belong to *me*. And as I said, *we* will have to mate completely before the unseelie come. Not you; *us*."

My anger swelled.

"You can't just skip every step in a relationship and expect me to happily jump in the sack with you," I snapped back, even though my chastisement was almost the literal definition of what I wanted to do. "You haven't even made it clear whether or not you *want me*. I may be trapped in this world, but that doesn't mean I'm going to permanently marry myself to some bastard who's offering to be my pity mate. I—"

His hands wrapped around my face, cupping my cheeks and cutting off my tirade.

"Wha—what are you doing?" My lips stumbled over the words.

His pelvis pressed against me, and the thick hardness of his erection dug into my abdomen.

He didn't say a damn thing as he tilted my head back with those hands on my cheeks.

My breathing picked up as his lips slowly lowered to mine.

Just before our mouths met, he growled, "I want you so damn badly I can't even *think*, Gorgeous."

Fire burned in his eyes a heartbeat before his lips captured mine. One of his hands dug into my hair, tightening in a handful of the dark silk. The other slid down to my ass, grabbing me and lifting me upward. When his erection met my center, I moaned.

Our kiss grew hotter, and more desperate.

My hands moved frantically over his chest and arms, feeling everything I could before the moment ended.

One of his remained in my hair, holding my face to his. The other slid beneath the fabric of my shorts, gripping a handful of my bare ass before sliding up toward the place I wanted it.

Just as his fingers brushed the slick wetness at my center, electricity raced through my skin. My back arched, and a gasp escaped me as my head crashed against the wall. Not a gasp of pleasure—one of shock, as I was yanked into one of my horrible dreams.

. . .

I STOOD in the middle of the forest, with ice on one side of me and fire on the other. The trees to my right were engulfed in the white-hot flames, and the sky was full of smoke.

Awful roars, growls, and screams pierced the air, and my arms wrapped around my stomach.

Not this again.

Not more blood.

I saw glimpses of the bodies around me before I could squeeze my eyes shut.

Priel's body.

His packs'.

The corpses of so many fae.

And off in the distance, there was still fighting.

The death wasn't enough.

It had never been enough.

These dreams had never felt completely like dreams, but they'd also never hit me in the middle of the day like this.

Was Priel right?

Was Vevol trying to communicate with me somehow?

"If you have something to say, just say it," I hissed at whoever or whatever had triggered the dream.

The air around me rippled, and when I peeked my eyes open, I realized that everything had changed.

I was now in the same location—a small clearing between the trees that was iced over on one side and not the other. But now the trees were looming over me, and the air both smelled and felt pure somehow.

"Polaris," a strange voice murmured behind me.

I spun around, and my eyes opened widely when I found myself face to face with a fae woman. She was almost as tall as the men, with the same pointed ears. Her hair was golden, her eyes a sparkling blue, and all she wore was the same fireproof tank top and shorts I had on. Glittering magical tattoos seemed to dance across every inch of her skin, constantly changing shape and color.

"Vevol?" I asked, stunned.

"Indeed."

In front of my eyes, her appearance shifted. She grew taller, her hair lightening and her eyes darkening.

I tried really hard not to gawk, but probably failed.

As soon as her appearance was settled, she began changing again. It was a total mind-warp to watch, but I supposed that as a goddess—or a whole world—she didn't really have to follow any rules.

"Have you been sending me the dreams? Was Priel right about that?" I asked, forcing my voice not to wobble.

"Your magic has the ability to tap into the futures of those around you. Most of your dreams have been triggered by your own wandering," she murmured.

Even her voice seemed to be changing as she added, "I cannot hold a form for long. Already, this drains me."

"Then why am I here? What have you been telling me?" I pleaded. I had seen so much fire and death, and I couldn't take much more of it.

"War is coming. The last time a fury like this one bloomed, it decimated the numbers of my women and forced the females into hiding." Her voice was soft and musical, and heart-wrenching as well somehow.

My lips parted. "There are female fae that were born here?"

"Not many, but yes. They remain beyond the lake your hound's portal opens and closes near. Only female fae can get past the boundary that protects them."

Fuck.

"Peace must be established. Until the future you see is free of the blood and flames your visions have shown you, the females must stay hidden." Her voice began to fade quickly, as did her form.

"Wait, how do I establish peace? How do we stop a war before it starts?" I rushed toward her, reaching for her hand.

"The Tame Queen," Vevol's voice whispered.

As if those last three words were a trigger, the dream ended suddenly.

EIGHT

I SAT UP QUICKLY, sucking in air frantically. My mind spun, my heart pounding wickedly-fast.

"Breathe," Mare said, her voice soft. Her hand was wrapped around my arm, her grip firm but not hard. She hadn't been in there when the dream—or vision—dragged me in, but I assumed some time had passed. A short vision could equate to an entire night's rest. Sometimes, even longer.

"Holy shit," I panted, my eyes slamming shut again.

"What happened?" Priel's snarl almost had me opening my eyes, but my head was still spinning so much that I thought I might vomit.

"Pretty sure I can see the future," I managed.

Okay, it was a lie.

I was confident that I could see the future.

Vevol *herself* had just told me I could see the damn future.

"I already knew that." His growl was fierce. "But you were out for hours, North. That can't be normal."

"Usually, I see things when I'm sleeping." I massaged my temple, feeling a harsh headache coming on as the dizziness started to calm down a little.

"Back off," Sunny snapped at Priel. "Give the girl some space."

His furious snarl told me it was time to intervene.

I finally opened my eyes, grabbing his wrist in one smooth motion and then yanking him toward me in a harsh one. My tug didn't really affect him, but he understood what I was trying to do and let me pull him over to me.

When he dropped down on the bed beside me, I set a hand on his knee to calm him down. His arm wrapped around my side, and he promptly dragged me over to him until we were practically glued together.

Well, then.

Sunny gave me a knowing smirk.

Mare fought a smile.

Dots wasn't in there. I knew she got triggered whenever someone grew angry or violent, so I wasn't surprised by her absence. Priel wasn't exactly the calm-angry kind of guy, which I appreciated, but not everyone was into that.

"What did you see?" Mare asked me.

"Vevol," I admitted. "The goddess, Vevol. She said..." I bit my lip, not sure what exactly I could and couldn't share.

Or what I *wanted* to share.

If I admitted to Priel that there were other women, there was a chance that he would stop wanting me. Fae chicks as tall and gorgeous as Vevol's constantly changing appearance was? No way could I compete with them.

On top of my selfish reasoning, there was also common sense. The less people who knew about the actual fae women before we figured out how to remove the war from our future, the better.

I needed to keep that shit quiet until things were settled.

And... maybe until I figured out whether or not Priel and I were really a thing. He had made some big claims, but I still wasn't completely sure that I believed him.

That was my selfishness talking again, but I didn't shut it up immediately. It was a part of me, as much as I refused to admit it aloud.

"She's been showing me these images because there's a war coming," I finally told them, gesturing to the walls. "Apparently I'm not as crazy as I thought."

Mare scowled. "We never thought you were crazy."

"Just pissed at the world, which is valid," Sunny offered.

I really appreciated hearing that, and shot her a grateful look.

"So how do we stop it?" Mare checked.

"She didn't really explain. Just said *'the Tame Queen'.*" I formed air quotes around the title with the hand that Priel hadn't captured.

"We'll need to cross the border, then," Sunny mused.

"No." Priel's voice was hard. "Not a fucking chance."

"There's no way the unseelies will allow their ladies to cross our borders either," a voice added from the doorway.

All of our attention jerked toward it, and I saw a grinning January standing there, with Lian behind her. His arm was wrapped possessively around her torso, which I thought was weird. Then again, the two of them were usually weird together.

January looked like a damned nature goddess, wearing a pair of dark green fireproof-underwear with all those gorgeous, golden tattoos shimmering over her strong, curvy body and her long, golden-brown hair falling to her ribs all cute-messy-like. I probably looked like a scarecrow that went rolling down a rocky hill in comparison, but refused to let myself consider that depressing fact.

My self-esteem could only take so much, after all.

"What did I miss?" January asked. "Why do we want to talk to the Tame Queen?"

Sunny and Mare looked at me.

I grimaced. "Apparently, I can see the future. Vevol—the goddess—told me that there's a war coming. When I asked her how to stop it, all she said was *'the Tame Queen'.*"

"Damn." January grimaced. "How are we going to get her away from her grump of a mate?"

"I can use her name," Lian said, like it was simple.

All of us ladies frowned.

January shot him an accusatory look and voiced all of our thoughts. "You know her name?"

He flashed her a small grin. "Everyone knows her name. She was the first female to come to our lands, and wasn't aware that she shouldn't share it."

"Damn." Her eyebrows lifted. "That sucks for her."

"Aev, the king, took to murdering anyone who used it, so no one dares anymore. But considering the alternative is attempting to cross their borders or calling a meeting, we'll have to take the risk," Lian mused.

"Maybe it won't be a risk at all." January's eyes gleamed as she looked at us. "I actually came back to tell you ladies something. I'm pregnant."

I blinked.

Suddenly the arm he had around her abdomen made a lot more sense.

Mare's eyes widened.

Sunny nearly choked on her own spit.

"Are we happy about this?" Dots called from outside the room.

January and Calian stepped in, letting her join the rest of us.

"We are," January confirmed.

"Then yay!" Dots threw her arms around the other woman, squeezing tightly. "Congrats."

"Thanks. I'm scared, but excited too," she confessed. "I realized we need to tell the other mated ladies, in case any of them are thinking about boning their mates. And one of them already did to stop the last potential war—so yeah, they need to know. If all of us ladies go alone, we could use the pregnancy as an excuse for taking advantage of her real name."

"Not a chance," Lian said smoothly.

"Fine, you can come," January grumbled.

"We can't bring any of the unmated females," Priel said from beside me, his voice clipped. "When Aev shows up, he'll try to drag all of them back with him. You know the bastard's still pissed that they're not all on his lands."

"Well, North has to come. She's the one who had the vision," January pointed out.

"North won't be unmated for long," Priel growled back.

There was a moment of silence.

"Why won't North be unmated for long?" January checked.

"Priel has decided that I'm his. We haven't agreed on that yet," I said, flashing him a look of warning.

He glared back at me, as if daring me to try to get away from him.

That was... an issue.

I wasn't sure how, exactly.

Or why.

Or what I'd do about it.

Because I wanted to be with him, but only if he wanted to be with me, and only if we actually started getting to know each other.

So, an issue.

An issue for tomorrow, though. Or next week. Or if I was lucky, next month.

"North's scars are actually something called brands. They mark her as ultra-powerful," Dots added helpfully. "So there are an assload of male fae who want her right now. She lied about being in love with Priel for the past year and a half to shut that down."

January's eyebrows shot up way into her forehead, and she looked at me. "Seriously?"

"Unfortunately." I grimaced.

Much of my grimacing was because my lie about Priel hadn't actually been a lie, and I felt kind of shitty for lying about lying, as ridiculous as that sounded.

"Damn."

"Yeah. I'll figure something out. I'm sure I'll come up with some way to fix the situation somehow," I said.

"Or we can just mate now and make things simple," Priel growled at me.

"Sure, if we want to start a war with the seelies before the unseelies take a stab at us," I shot back.

"Sounds worth it to me." He flashed me a feral grin.

I scowled. "You're dead in every violent vision I've seen, so you should probably change your tune."

"All of these bastards are too happy to go to war. They need something to focus on that isn't four single chicks and fighting," January said with a sigh.

"*Three* single chicks," Priel corrected, tugging me closer.

"We still haven't agreed on that," I grumbled back.

"Not shoving a fae dude away from you is usually enough agreement for them." January grinned at me. "You'll get used to it."

Shit, I hoped so.

Because I still had the most ridiculous fluttering in my stomach every time Priel touched me. Or looked at me. Or... pretty much did anything, honestly.

"You *do* have to come with us to talk to the Tame Queen, regardless of whatever you two figure out," January said, waving a hand toward me.

"There's no way around that," I agreed.

Priel growled again, releasing me and standing smoothly. His fists clenched, flames engulfing the tensed skin, ink, and muscles as he began pacing the room.

"I think we'll give you guys a minute to talk," January said, eyeing the pissed-off hound.

She and Calian stepped away, and the other girls followed them out. Dots gave me a thumbs-up and Sunny, a saucy grin.

The door closed behind them, and it was just me and Priel.

I bit my lip, not sure what to say. I definitely wasn't getting up off of my bed unless I figured that one out. The bed was safe, since Priel currently wasn't on it.

The hound continued to pace, his body tense and his expression furious.

My stomach clenched when I realized that one of the paintings featuring a strip of his abdomen and tattoos would be directly within his line of sight if he looked up from the tile he was glaring down at. It blended in with the colors of the gory picture I'd hidden it on the edge of, but it was undeniably Priel.

Don't look up.

Don't look up.

Don't look u—

His eyes lifted.

He halted.

Shit.

I could practically see the gears turning in his mind, even though I could only see the back of his head.

I'd done my best to hide the evidence of my scandalous dreams within the paintings, but that one was one of the clearest images. If you looked closely, there was absolutely no denying it.

His gaze slowly moved off of that painting, and across the walls.

I squeezed my eyes shut, knowing exactly what he would see.

An image of our intertwined hands, pressing against a mattress together.

A small painting of his large, inked hand stretched over my brand-dotted abdomen, which had a few tattoos of its own.

Bits and pieces of the art on his body, embedded in every shadow I'd painted.

In my room, Priel was *everywhere.*

The bed groaned, and my eyes flew open just in time to see Priel step behind my headboard, crouching down so he could see the paintings I'd hidden there.

I opened my mouth to give him an explanation, to figure out a way to lie to him, but failed.

Nothing came out.

I knew exactly what he was seeing; how many times had I done exactly what he just had?

Hundreds.

I did it every day.

I'd slide behind the bed frame, into the gap that I'd left there, and lower myself to the floor. And, crouched in that little space, I'd stare at the glimpse of the life of my literal dreams.

Most of them, I could ignore. I didn't paint everything I saw; I would never be able to. The dreams were too full, too dynamic.

But the image I'd painted behind my bed was one I had never been able to get out of my mind.

It wasn't anything epic or important.

It was a view from the side of me sitting on a chair, with a wall covered in gorgeous, painted landscapes visible behind me. Not the wall in Priel's cave that I'd visited—I'd never dreamed of that place before—but a different one.

My hair was at least six inches shorter, and all I had on was a fireproof tank and shorts. Instead of black, they were made of the same colorful fabric on Priel's practically-trademarked shorts.

Priel was kneeling on the floor between my parted legs, one of his hands holding the magical tattoo gun near my abdomen, and the other draped over my thigh.

At the moment of the painting, he wasn't actually inking me. Instead, he was grinning up at me, having just told me a joke. I was laughing, one of my palms resting on his shoulder and the other on top of the hand he had on my thigh.

I wasn't sure what about the image meant so much to me. Maybe the simplicity, or the mundaneness. Or maybe it was just the look of pure happiness on my face, and the devoted humor on Priel's.

Whatever it was, I had yearned for that moment so damn much that words couldn't even describe the ache.

I hadn't known it was the future I was seeing.

I hadn't even known that my dreams were possible.

I'd chalked it up to an overactive imagination and hero worship for the gorgeous man who had brought me supplies when I'd first woken up in Vevol.

And now...

Shit.

Was that moment actually possible?

What if Priel and I could really get to that moment I'd painted?

Fear clutched my abdomen.

I didn't even really know the man. Sure, I'd been crushing on him hard core, the sex dreams were unreal, and things had gotten intense between us on one occasion.

But none of those things meant I was ready to throw myself into the kind of serious relationship he would want. Or even the kind that I'd painted. I could be on board with some hot sex, but everything else? I had no idea how to be in a relationship.

I'd barely survived the arranged one my parents set up.

I jerked to my feet.

Priel was still behind the headboard, so this was probably my last chance for escape.

I couldn't leave the Stronghold, and I didn't want to.

But... I needed space.

Air.

I hurried to the bathroom, shutting the door behind myself and locking it quickly before I collapsed to the ground. My ass didn't appreciate the hard tile beneath me, but I ignored the discomfort.

My eyes squeezed shut when I heard Priel's footsteps in my room.

Maybe I needed space, but he'd made it pretty clear a little earlier that *he* did *not*.

There was a bit of pressure against the door, and when he spoke, I heard his low voice not far above my head.

He must've been sitting on the other side.

"How long have you been seeing us together?" the words were soft, and so much gentler than I expected.

I bit my lip, not sure how to answer without pissing him off or making him think I was ready for more than I actually was.

I debated it silently for a while before I settled on, "I thought they were just dreams."

"North." He knew exactly what I was doing.

There wasn't much of a point to beating around the bush, so I stopped.

"Since we met."

"Fuck." His hiss didn't bode well for me.

My stomach clenched. "Nothing is set in stone. The future probably changes all the time. It's not like you have no choice; you can still pick someone else. We're not—"

He quickly growled, "I'm furious that I didn't pursue you sooner, not angry with you. There is no one else for me; there never has been, and there never will be. As far as I'm concerned, those things you saw are our future. Period."

Oh.

Wow.

A long, charged silence followed.

I finally whispered, "We don't even know each other."

"That's easily remedied."

He wasn't wrong.

"I'm not ready to promise anything," I added.

"I don't need a promise; I've seen your future. And it belongs to *me.*"

A shiver rolled down my spine. "You're so possessive."

"Incredibly." His growled agreement made me bite my lip. "Now, I need you to come out here and let me hold you in my arms while you tell me every single thing I missed while I was outside. I'm fucking losing it, if you haven't noticed."

I laughed softly. "I noticed."

"So come out here and fix that for me."

I bit my lip to stop myself from smiling, but didn't move to get up. My humor faded into a wall of serious hesitancy. "You didn't tell me how you felt about seeing us together like that in my painting."

There was a long pause.

He finally admitted, "I felt like I wished there was a way to skip right to that moment and get lost in it, with you. You still don't believe that I want you, do you?"

"I don't know," I whispered. "I know that you think I'm yours, and that I want you to be mine. But I didn't really live much, on Earth. My parents didn't let me leave our house very often, and I was barely nineteen when I was brought here. They thought they were protecting me, and I love them for that, but I always felt isolated. I'm not good with people, because of it. And I have a hard time with trust."

"Well, I'll do whatever it takes to make my desire for you constantly and annoyingly clear until you're certain about it, then."

My lips curved upward a bit. "What would that entail?"

"Kissing. Touching. Talking. Complimenting. Snuggling. Licking. Stroking. Petting. Sniffing. And fucking, in every way there is."

My face heated.

"Of course, that's only when you're willing, Gorgeous."

Taking the opportunity to change the subject, I scoffed at the nickname. "You have got to come up with something better to call me than that."

He chuckled. "Give me your full name, and maybe I will."

I bit my lip, considering it.

If I gave him my name, he'd be able to call me to him, wherever he was. It would be dangerous, but in some ways, safer too. If I were ever captured, or taken, or attacked...

Alright, maybe it wasn't such a terrible idea.

I still hesitated, though.

Honestly, I trusted him. He had fought outside the Stronghold for months, keeping me safe from the other fae who wanted me as their mate. Even if his reasons were selfish—because he'd claimed that he wanted me as his, even then—that wasn't something I could just forget or pretend hadn't happened.

He fought for me.

And I trusted him.

And damn, I liked kissing him.

"Everyone on Earth always called me North," I admitted, my voice barely above a whisper. "My parents gave me a unique name, but it was *too* unique, hence the nickname."

He waited.

I sighed softly. "My real name is Polaris. It's another name for a star we can pretty much always see on Earth, called the North Star. Hence my nickname."

"Polaris," Priel mused.

There was a slight tingle at the base of my spine when the word left his lips.

I changed the subject again, not wanting to get emotional if the topic began to revolve around my parents. "Let's make something to eat. I'm hungry."

Priel was standing when I opened the door between us. He offered me a hand, but I didn't take it, stepping past him.

A low chuckle escaped him, and he caught my arm with a smooth palm that wrapped around my wimpy bicep.

"Like it or not, female, you're mine now," he murmured to me. "And I'm going to make you so damn happy about that, you won't even know what to do with yourself."

I shot him a raised eyebrow. "I'll believe that when I see it."

His response was a scorching grin that had me fighting a wave of said happiness.

NINE

JANUARY AND LIAN were already cooking when we stepped out of my room, so when they invited us to wait and eat with everyone else, we headed to the couch on the far side of the room. Mare was reading close by, and Sunny and Dots were watching a chick flick I knew they had seen a hundred times already. Priel's intrigued gaze followed the screen as we passed it.

It occurred to me that the man probably had no idea how human relationships worked. It was probably going to be a long shot, trying to help him understand that I wanted to get to know him a little first instead of just jumping into the gloriously-hot sex I'd seen us having. But sex would mate us permanently, and despite what I'd seen and felt thus far, I wanted us to be on the same page about most things before we took that step.

"Hey," Mare murmured, as I sat down near her. Priel sat on my other side, his arm wrapping around my waist. His fingers dug into my hip, and my face heated when I realized I hadn't put my long-sleeved shirt and pants on.

"Hey," I mirrored her greeting, though I focused on the movie for a few minutes.

When I saw her start moving a little, I glanced over and saw her wiping her eyes a bit. They looked like they'd been watering—but why was she crying?

"What's wrong?" I whispered.

"Oh, nothing." She flashed me a small, watery smile. "I'm just reading poetry. From what I've gathered, this book came from another world that's connected to Earth, and some of the poems are really emotional. I've never read anything like them before. This is my seventh or eighth read-through, but they still get me."

It didn't surprise me that there were other worlds connected to Earth, given where we currently were.

"I'll have to read them sometime," I said, and the smile she flashed me grew wider.

Maybe talking about books was the key to Mare's heart.

SOON AFTER THE conversation about the poems, the food was ready, and we all gathered and ate together. It was strange, having a family dinner of sorts, but in a way that made my heart happier than I knew how to deal with at that point.

After we'd eaten, cleaned up, and chatted for a bit, Priel scooped me up into his arms as he stood smoothly. I yelped as my feet left the ground, and scowled at him when he grinned at me and started moving. He stopped at the bookshelf to grab the poetry book Mare and I had been talking about—which she'd finished reading through again during the movie—then carried me back to my room.

"What are you doing?" I grumbled at him.

"Reading poems from another world while spending time holding my woman." He shut the door behind him. "My portals have never taken me anywhere other than Earth, as far as I've been able to tell. I'm curious about their poetry."

That was an understandable sort of curiosity, I supposed.

Priel set me down in the middle of my mattress. There was a burned spot on one of the blankets, thanks to me, but he had flipped it around so the burn was near our feet. The book hit the mattress beside me, and then the fae was sliding into the bed, pulling my blankets over us.

"I need some of those fireproof plants in here," I mumbled, as he rolled me up onto my side and tucked his front up against my back.

"I'll get some as soon as I can," he agreed.

I tried not to let him notice the way I sucked in a breath when his thick arm wrapped around my abdomen.

He was propped up a little awkwardly on one arm—and opened the book with the hand connected to that arm—but when he buried his nose in my neck, he growled in approval.

He also gave me way too many damned goosebumps.

I forced my eyes to follow the words on the page. They were either in English, or Vevol's magic had translated them for me.

I'd never really been a poem girl, but I tried to enjoy the writing. Some of it didn't make sense, but most of it did.

After we made it through a dozen or so, I closed my eyes and just enjoyed the peace of the moment.

I'd never been held like this before. I'd never had a man's arms around me so possessively. I'd never felt so... important to him.

My father's protectiveness was mostly to blame for that.

Wistfulness engulfed me as I thought about the family I'd left behind. They weren't good for me, or for my future, but they were mine, and I had loved them. I hoped like hell that my sister was okay, that she was coping with losing me. We hadn't ever been super close, and she'd moved out a few years before I was brought to Vevol, but still, I worried for her.

Priel's nose remained buried in my hair, his chest rising and falling steadily against my back. His fingers were curled beneath my hip, getting trapped underneath me, but his thumb traced a slow circle just above the place his fingers had disappeared to.

Priel read through many more poems before he lingered on one much longer than the others.

I peeked my eyes open to see what had captured his attention, and found a poem titled *I Burn for You* by someone named Orthrus.

My gaze followed the words, and my throat swelled a bit as I read them.

· · ·

SITTING BENEATH THE SHINING MOON, I burn; I burn for you.

Leaning against this wall of stone, I blaze, waiting for you.

Standing under this sky of stars, I watch while my flames dance for you.

Walking up a road of ash, I smoke, searching for you.

Drowning in the pain of flesh, I'm blazing, flaming, smoking, and burning... for you.

THERE WAS SO much emotion in the words that it choked me up a little. I didn't know what had inspired them, or why, but I wanted to.

Priel held the book open for a few more long moments before he set it down on the mattress.

The arm he had beneath me wrapped around my chest, dragging me as close as I could possibly get to him.

"I want to know you," he murmured to me. "Tell me everything."

"How am I supposed to tell you *everything*?" I asked, my eyes shutting as I leaned back against Priel's chest.

"I suppose you'll just have to spend the next few months lying in this bed with me until you've spoken all of it."

I snorted, and felt his lips stretch in a grin against my neck.

"Why don't *you* tell *me* everything?" I countered.

"Sure. It won't take long." His hand slid out from beneath my hip, his fingertips dragging over my abdomen slowly. My body warmed in response to his touch, but I didn't acknowledge it.

He began softly. "There's not much to do in Vevol, other than fighting, cooking, and creating art. I know men on Earth often fulfill different roles than the women there, but here, we do everything. Cleaning. Sewing. Cooking. Gardening. That was my life. I painted. Inked my brothers. Grew plants, in a patch hidden away from the other hellhounds. Life was simple, but dull. When the itch got too bad, I started fights, or joined the ones already happening. Life had no purpose, then, and a life without purpose isn't much of a life. Since I started fighting for you, you became that purpose. And now, everything has changed."

"Is that a good thing, though?" I asked.

"It's an *incredible* thing." His hand still stroked my abdomen lightly. My body throbbed with his touch, but I did my best to ignore the feelings. Nothing had ever felt so intimate... or so safe.

It was my turn to tell him about my life, I supposed.

My voice was at least as soft as his. "My parents were good to me, but they were terrible people. They killed in cold blood, hurt other people for the sake of money, and manipulated with every breath they took. They matched me to some guy in an arranged marriage the day I turned eighteen," I admitted.

His body stilled. "Marriage?"

"Yes, the human version of mating."

His fingers wrapped tightly around my hip.

"I didn't marry him. The whole thing was a long, drawn-out attempt to make a statement to my parents. The other family was going to kill me. When I heard them talking about what they were going to do with me, I waited until they were near a forest, and then threw myself out of the car. It was like... jumping off a running hellhound, I guess. But humans are a lot more fragile than fae. I got horribly injured in the process, and ended up spending a few days hiding out in the forest. Almost died a few different times. When my family finally found me, I was taken to a hospital, and ended up spending about a month healing there," I admitted.

Priel was stiff behind me. Really damn stiff.

"Anyway, I survived, but I realized I needed to find a way out of my parents' world. The problem was, there wasn't one. They had the money, the property, and everything I would need to get away from them. When I asked them to let me leave, they said no, and warned me that they'd have to hunt me down if I ran, for my own safety. They didn't give me the scars on my body, but as much as I hate to admit it, their choices were sort of the reason for the physical and mental reminders. And yet they still weren't willing to let me go."

"The day I wished on those candles..." I swallowed roughly. "I didn't want to leave them. I loved them; I still do. They're brutal, harsh, and terrible in some ways, but they were mine, and for that, they had my complete loyalty. I still feel guilty for making that wish, for leaving them."

"They didn't deserve you," Priel said, his voice low in my ear.

"Maybe not, but they had me anyway."

His hands stroked my hip, and we both grew quiet for a few minutes, lost in our own minds.

When I finally spoke up again, I was nervous. A little nauseous, too.

"If I let myself fall in love with you, it won't be soft and gentle, Priel. I don't love that way. When I care about something, or someone, I dig my claws into their skin and I hold on like the alternative would be my end. I don't love lightly, or sweetly. You would get all of me. The shitty, angry parts. The scared, furious parts. The intense, obsessive parts. I don't love many people, but when I love, it can be brutal, like the bastards who raised me."

"Then I look forward to feeling your claws in my skin, Polaris." His teeth brushed my throat, and I shivered. "And I can assure you that you will be loved just as fiercely as you love, should you let me in."

My throat swelled.

"Tell me about painting. When did you begin?" His hand stroked my hip.

"When I was little, I used to draw on everything..."

PRIEL and I stayed in my bed for hours, talking. We didn't touch intimately, or even kiss. But the conversations we shared, the stories we traded, were worth more than orgasms to me.

And as much as I'd fought it in the beginning, I was pretty sure that I was going to fall in love with that bastard.

The silences between stories were thick and comfortable, like a massive blanket. After one pause, I murmured, "Priel?"

He was silent.

When I paid attention to the rise and fall of his chest, I realized he was breathing evenly.

Happiness slid through me with that realization. The first day I was in his cave, I had thought it was an insult that he fell asleep so easily in my presence. Now, I knew it was a privilege that I relaxed him so completely.

I needed to pee, though, so I carefully eased myself away from him. It took a little time, but I finally made it out from underneath his thick, heavy limbs.

After I used the bathroom, I studied the man in my bed. He looked so peaceful.

My mind went back to the words of the poem we'd found.

I burn for you.

I was feeling a bit overwhelmed by the intensity of my emotions, so I slipped out of my room for just a few minutes, leaving Priel asleep on my bed with one last long, backward glance.

My eyes scanned the living room. Everyone seemed to have gone to bed, except Mare.

I padded over to her, taking a seat on the other side of the couch. My legs slid up onto the cushions, and I wrapped my arms around them.

"You okay?" she murmured to me.

The question caught me off guard.

Was I okay?

For the first time in a long time, I actually *did* feel okay, despite everything.

"I think I am," I admitted.

Her lips curved upward, just slightly. "You seem happy."

Honestly?

I thought maybe I was that, too.

"Can I ask you something?" I wondered.

She shrugged one shoulder. "Is it about sex with the fae?"

I snorted. "Definitely not."

She closed her book, leaving a finger between a few of the pages. "Then go ahead."

"You read a lot. If this world were one of your books, how would we prevent the war that I've seen coming? Vevol said the Tame Queen is the answer, but I don't know how she could prevent the hell I've seen from breaking loose."

Mare grimaced. "If there were more women, it would knock the tension of the situation down a lot, and probably kill the potential of a war. Even one woman to every five or six fae could improve things tremendously. But with four of us to a couple hundred unseelie fae, the odds aren't in anyone's favor. If we could combine forces with the rest of the humans, there would be twenty of us women. According to Ana, there are around six hundred fae in this world. I don't know where she got the information, but it seems accurate from what I've seen."

I grimaced.

The situation just kept getting worse.

Vevol's words came to my mind.

There were fae women, hidden away on an island.

"Can you keep a secret?" I asked her.

She flashed me a smile. "Of course."

I lowered my voice, leaning closer to her. She leaned in too.

"There are fae women hidden away," I whispered.

Her eyes widened. "What?"

"Vevol told me that the fighting got so bad between the fae that the women had to separate from them. I think she must've wiped their memories about it or something."

"Holy shit," she breathed.

"Yeah. The women have to stay hidden until we can de-escalate things between the fae, though. The seelies and unseelies have had issues for so long that she says we can't risk the fae ladies."

"Wow." Mare sat back, running a hand over the top of her head. Her hair was up in a poof, like it often was. "So we just need to talk to the Tame Queen and figure out how to stop the fae from fighting."

"And how to introduce a group of who-knows-how-many female fae into a group of emotionally-scarred ex-human women and horny single men," I agreed.

"Shit." She bit her lip, excitement in her eyes. "You have to go talk to the Queen, and the sooner, the better. If you leave before the sun comes up, I think you can get away from the other men before they decide how they really feel about you declaring your love for Priel."

I nodded.

She had a point.

"I'll wake him up, and he'll figure out a way to break me out of here."

She smiled. "I'll let Lian and January know where you're headed so they can meet up with you too."

"Thanks." I gave her a quick, if hesitant smile of my own. "I know I've been a nightmare to live with, and I'm sorry."

She brushed a hand through the air. "We all understand. Always have. For some of us, this place is a miracle. For others, it's a prison." Her words were simple, but they made my throat swell up.

I jerked my head in a nod.

It had felt like a prison for too long. With the terrible dreams, and the lust for someone I'd never even really talked to, and...

Shit.

That was a lot to think about.

I pushed the thoughts away.

Things in Vevol were going to change for the better. I was going to make sure of it.

The door to my room crashed open, and I lifted my eyes to a wild-eyed Priel. His shoulders were tense, one of his fists burning as he looked around the room.

Our gazes collided, and his body relaxed instantly.

The fire on his hand went out, and he dragged it through his already-wild blond hair. "You scared the shit out of me."

"Sorry." I stood up as I apologized, mouthing a 'thank-you' to Mare. She only grinned in response.

Ten

WHEN I REACHED HIM, he dragged me into his arms, closing the door behind me and then pinning me to it. His gigantic arms landed on the door above my head, his forehead tilting toward me. Mine leaned back, and he stopped when our lips were a breath away from each other.

"What were you doing, Polaris?"

Whew, my full name sounded a hell of a lot sexier coming from his lips than it ever had from anyone else's.

"Mare and I came up with a plan," I admitted, lifting my hands and placing them on his bare chest.

"What kind of plan?"

"The kind where I admit that I know I'm eventually going to agree to be your mate and convince you to run away with me in the middle of the night."

His lips curved upward wickedly. "I like this plan already."

"I figured." I closed my eyes.

He surprised me by brushing his lips against mine, lightly, and then murmuring, "Continue."

My eyes remained closed. I was enjoying the moment too much to open them. "You and I are going to sneak out tonight to find the unseelie queen. January and Lian will catch up and join us."

Priel's lips brushed against mine again. "I'd like this plan better if it didn't include another couple."

"The goal is to avoid a war so you don't end up dead, remember? You can sacrifice a little alone time for the sake of your survival."

He chuckled quietly. "I suppose."

His lips brushed mine yet again.

I was enjoying the contact too much, and opened my eyes. "I'm not ready for us to become full-on mates yet, okay?"

"There's lots of fun to be had even without completing the bond though, isn't there?" The gleam in his eyes was wicked.

"Yes. But..." I trailed off when his lips lowered to my throat.

My fingers dug into his chest as he sucked lightly on the skin beneath my ear.

"What else have you seen of our future, Polaris?" he murmured between sucks on my skin.

The words died in my throat as he moved down the sensitive column.

Had I not told him that my dreams were pretty much full of sex?

"North?" he murmured, dragging his teeth over my collarbone and making me shudder.

"Ask me again after we're far enough away from all of the horny bastards outside," I whispered, buying myself some time.

Something told me that if he found out I'd been dreaming about him naked, he would probably *get* naked a lot more often.

And I wasn't so sure I was ready for a naked Priel who actually wanted me.

Yeah, it had been awesome when he was bare and insane in his shower and in his bed, but that was back before I knew he wanted to make things permanent between us. With the possibility of that permanence looming over my head, I was more uncertain.

It was one thing to lust after a guy for months on end.

It was a totally *different* thing to pledge your forever to said guy.

"You're ready to get out of here?" he murmured to me, still exploring my collarbone with his lips, teeth, and tongue. "I'd be more than happy to spread you out on that bed and taste every inch of you first."

Heat flared within me.

Hot damn, that sounded good.

Restrain, North.

"That's probably not a good i—" I breathed in sharply when his lips dragged further down my chest, closer to my boobs. "Priel." I shoved his face away, and he let me push him a couple of inches. "We're not doing this here. No one likes being woken up by the sound of someone else having sex."

He flashed me a wicked grin. "Is that what we would be doing?"

"I'm serious," I said, though I fought a grin of my own.

"Alright, I'll sneak us out of here. You'll have to ride on my back though, in case anyone hears us."

"Fine." I huffed out a breath.

Honestly, I'd kind of been looking forward to another run in my hellhound form.

"When we're sure we've gotten away from them, you can shift too."

Well, that was a deal.

"Alright. How do we get out?"

"Back door." He gestured over his shoulder.

I blinked.

There was a back door?

He flashed me another grin. "Nev and Teris installed it while they were here fixing the hole in January's ceiling a few months back. Figured one of us might need a secret entrance or escape one of these days."

I sighed. "I should question that, but I really don't want to."

"Good." He brushed his lips against my forehead before bending down and tugging me onto his back. I bit back a shriek as he stood smoothly, my arms wrapping around his neck.

"I am way too old for a piggy-back ride," I whisper-complained to him as he strode out of the room.

"When you get to be as ancient as me, you realize you're never too old for anything that you find fun," he whispered back.

I grimaced. "Don't remind me how old you are."

He snorted. "Alright."

He padded down the hallway—I waved at Mare as we passed the living room—and then stopped at a wall at the hallway's end that I was certain was just a wall. Reaching up to the place it met the ceiling, he paused for a moment.

Suddenly and silently, the wall slid down, opening up to the forest.

I gawked.

Secret entrance.

The younger version of me who was obsessed with Harry Potter would've squealed.

The older, jaded version of me only squealed on the inside.

Priel stepped outside, then placed his hand back on the wall. His magic kicked in, and it slid shut once again.

I watched in awe until he spun us around and began to jog silently into the forest. The way he could run without making a sound was incredibly impressive.

When I opened my mouth to ask him how the secret door's magic worked, he reached back and put a hand to my mouth, covering it.

Shit.

Right.

There were probably fae on the other side of the Stronghold, camped out and waiting to see what happened next. Or possibly fighting, even after my threat.

We needed to be quiet.

Good thing Priel was there, because I was absolutely not stealthy on my own.

Priel picked up the pace as we got further from the other fae.

When he'd been running for half an hour or so, he finally shifted. A shiver ran down my spine and an electric shock sizzled over my skin as his form stretched and changed. My whole body seemed to relax as I draped over his extremely-solid back, my arms still looped around his neck but no longer connecting at the middle.

The forest seemed to fly around us, and my eyelids grew heavy as it did. Falling asleep on the back of a hellhound probably wasn't the smartest thing I'd ever do, but I hadn't gotten around to sleeping that night, so I was exhausted.

Priel's fire curled over my skin as if whispering to me that he had me, and slowly, my eyes shut and I drifted off.

DELICIOUS HEAT ENGULFED ME.

A gasp escaped me, and my fingers dug into the sheets on the bed.

Priel's bed, in a cave I hadn't been to; I recognized the feel and smell of it from my past dreams.

His hands were wrapped around my ass and thighs, spreading me wide for him as I sat on his face, rocking and panting and making noises I'd only ever made in my dreams of us.

His teeth caught my clit, and an orgasm cut through me so sharply I almost screamed. My body trembled, pleasure burning me whole.

Fire blazed around us without burning the sheets or bed. I couldn't tell whether it was mine or Priel's—and it didn't matter.

Not when he was unraveling me, his face buried in my core and his fingers teasing my entrance.

"Fuck," I panted down to him.

Though I was living the moment, it wasn't mine. The words hadn't come from my own conscious decision to speak; they were a part of the future I was seeing.

The dream version of me breathed, "I want you inside me."

"You're not begging yet," Priel growled into my core, slowly rubbing his prickly chin over my sensitive skin.

I fought a cry that threatened to escape at the overwhelming feel of it.

"Or giving me orders." He nuzzled my clit with his nose, and I bucked a little. A gravelly chuckle escaped him as he slid a thick finger inside me slowly, blowing lightly on my sensitive bits. "I haven't even finished warming you up yet."

"Then get to work," I shot back, burying my fingers in his hair and tugging on the strands.

His grin stretched against my center, his teeth nipping lightly at my clit again. "Yes ma'am."

A second finger slid inside me as he slowly began stroking me with his tongue, taking his sweet time. He knew it was better for me that way—with the buildup.

His fingers moved lazily within me, dragging over my g-spot now and again like they were oblivious to the way I needed the touches.

They weren't oblivious. He just wanted me needy and wrecked when we were done, like he always did. It would be incredible, like it always was. He would make sure of that.

"Stop teasing," I panted, desperation beginning to clutch me.

"Or what?" my hellhound growled wickedly.

"I'll kill you," I hissed.

"You can do better than that, Gorgeous."

"I'll ink one of my brands," I shot back.

A possessive snarl escaped him, and shit, he ravaged me.

Pleasure swelled within me.

My expression contorted.

MY HEAD JERKED UPWARD, and I found Priel crouched over me, worry lining his forehead. His fingers pressed to my throat, checking my pulse and finding my heart beating wildly.

Molten-hot need burned in my veins.

I was so close—so damn close.

I would combust if I didn't lose it.

My hand slipped into my shorts.

Priel's eyes dilated as he realized what was going on.

He ripped my shorts down my thighs, watching me drag my fingers over my clit. A moment later, he'd ripped my hand away and replaced it with his tongue.

The feeling was like nothing I'd ever experienced. It was incredible in my dreams, but the dreams weren't happening to me in that moment. Nothing in my visions felt real, or nearly as intense as it was supposed to.

This—his tongue on my clit, while his hands opened my thighs —was real.

And *shit*, it was intense.

I cried out as I lost control, rocking against his mouth while I gripped handfuls of his hair like a lifeline. He snarled at me, feasting on me while I shattered.

Heavy panting shook my whole body as I started coming down from the high. My fingers still clutched his hair, but he didn't even slow down.

Damn.

This version of Priel didn't know my body. He didn't understand what I needed, or wanted.

"Slow, first," I panted to him.

His flaming eyes lifted from my body long enough to meet mine.

"Start slow, then build up," I explained quickly, still struggling for air.

When he lowered his lips back to my core, the drag of his tongue was so excruciatingly slow that my body literally quaked.

"Holy shit," I moaned, as he continued the slow, hot assault.

His flames wrapped around my body, heating me in every way there was.

When he started picking up the pace, I was a goner. I arched and cried out, the way I had in my dreams, and the pleasure was so incredible it almost hurt.

The man looked really damn proud of himself when I looked up at him, my head still spinning and his tongue still moving in those slow, toe-curling strokes.

His movements were slow for a few blissfully-hot minutes, his eyes studying me closely as he began to pick up the pace again.

This time, when my breathing grew shallow, he slid a thick finger inside me.

He didn't know exactly where to touch me, unlike in my dreams. But in our reality, I was just as much of a beginner as he was. I didn't know where he should rub his fingertip or knuckle any more than he did.

But it still felt incredible.

My parents had been super controlling in more ways than I cared to admit. I'd never had a vibrator or anything similar; they would've found it and taken it away in a heartbeat. The closest I'd ever gotten to this moment was with my own fingers, and they were skinny little bitches. The way Priel's monstrous one felt inside me... it was unreal.

"Shit," I moaned, when he added another finger, still working my clit with his tongue.

It made me feel so insanely *full*, in ways I'd never even imagined.

Probably a good call, to start with the fingers. I was so tight I would've cut his damn—

All thoughts ceased when he nipped at my clit for the first time.

The arching and cries repeated, but feeling myself squeeze around his fingers as I lost it was a whole new level of incredible.

I came down from the high panting again.

"Need to stop," I groaned at Priel, when he still didn't pull away from me.

He finally dragged his tongue away from my clit, but left his fingers buried inside my throbbing heat.

"Here, let me touch you." I reached for the erection I could most definitely see raging against the seam of his shorts.

I didn't know exactly what I was doing when it came to his cock, but I'd seen myself touch him so many times that I was pretty sure I could replicate what he liked.

"You don't have to," he growled at me, catching my outstretched hand with his free one and lacing his fingers through mine. His other hand was still buried inside me, and I was enjoying it so much that I hoped he wouldn't try to take them out yet. "This was more than enough."

"I want to, though."

It was the honest truth.

I didn't want to feel like I'd received more than I'd given. I wanted to return the favor, to make sure he knew that the feelings were mutual.

"Polaris," he warned me, as I untangled my fingers from his and reached for the waistband of his shorts. He undid the strange, hidden button for me, but made no move to take them off.

"Stop trying to talk me out of it," I shot back.

His lips curved upward slightly.

The bastard always liked my sass in my dreams, too.

"Help me out here," I told him, tugging on his shorts. He grunted at me, but dragged them down a few inches right afterward.

His erection popped free, and I just stared at it for a moment. It was even bigger than I remembered, and it was slick.

I realized he'd already lost control once.

Shit, that made me feel sexy.

My hand wrapped around him, and he let out a low growl.

I watched myself stroke him slowly, using his release to slide smoothly over his length. His whole damn body tensed, the fingers he had inside me curling a bit.

His thumb found my clit even as his eyes shut and his jaw clenched, the fire around us growing hotter and more desperate.

The pleasure within me rose to new heights as I watched the sexy hellhound struggle with control before he finally snarled and pumped into my fist, losing it completely. I shattered with him, crying out as the orgasm cut through me. The flames on his skin blazed over both of us as he throbbed in my grip, the evidence of his pleasure coating my thigh as he dropped down beside me. Our chests both heaved, mine still covered by my tank top. His fire flared over my leg and his cock, and I felt the wetness disappear from my skin.

Satisfaction had me sagging against him, even though he didn't remove his fingers from my body.

"Ever planning on letting go?" I murmured to him.

"Not until you make me."

His mumble made me smile.

"Who were you dreaming about?" His growl a few moments later was a little feral, and I loved that.

"You. I always dream about you." The words slipped out too easily, and I bit my lip, worried how he would react.

"You'd fucking better." His fingers stroked my inner walls, and I sucked in a breath when I realized he'd found my g-spot without any help from me. "Was that your first sex dream about us?"

I snorted. "*Hell* no."

His gravelly chuckle made me grin out at the forest around us. "You'd better start sharing the details so I know how to compete with my future self."

I bit my lip to stop my grin from widening. "I guess I could do that."

Maybe I should've told him about my dreams earlier.

Eleven

After a few more minutes, Priel reluctantly told me that we needed to get moving again. We both shifted, then, and hit the road. Er, dirt.

Partway through the morning, a phoenix and a massive gray dragon caught up to us. They stayed above us in the air until we slowed down, and I realized we were approaching a thick stone building. It was shaped strangely, but I couldn't tell what exactly it was supposed to resemble from the ground.

"Welcome to the borders between our land and the unseelies'," Priel told me, his arm sliding around my waist. His hand landed on my abdomen possessively, and I found myself wrapping my arm around his bicep.

January and Lian landed on their feet a short distance away from us, and she flashed me a wicked grin. "Ready to wreak some havoc?"

I couldn't stop myself from mirroring her expression. "Why the hell not?"

"You guys need to stay behind us," she told Lian and Priel, as she looped her arm through my free one. "No one will try to kill us, but you're probably free game."

"Our lives are connected," Lian reminded her. "They won't kill me."

All three of us looked at Priel.

"I'm not hiding behind you," he growled back.

I sighed.

Of course he wouldn't.

It wasn't even worth the debate.

"Let's get this over with. We need to change the future." I tightened my grip on Priel's arm, and January let go of me so we could walk to the building. The snow melted beneath all of our feet as we went, exposing dirt and rocks that didn't affect my fae toes at all.

There was no furniture inside; just a large, open room that I could now see was shaped like a triangle. The walls and floors were the same cold, gray stone, and there were no windows to allow us a peek out at either the seelie or unseelie portions of the land.

"So what's the plan?" January asked me.

I grimaced. "We use the queen's name to get her here, tell her what Vevol told me, and hope for the best."

January's eyebrows shot upward. "Damn."

"Yep."

I looked at Priel, who looked at Lian.

"Naomi," he said aloud. "We need to speak with you."

I felt a wave of magic roll through the room.

The air shimmered wildly, and then a woman stepped through the glittering strip. She was slim, with perfect-looking wavy dark hair, and pale skin. There were magical tattoos all over her hands, and she wore a bell-shaped, long-sleeve sweater dress with tights beneath it. Compared to her, the rest of us probably looked homeless.

Her eyes were narrowed as she took in the building around us, but they softened slightly when she saw January.

"Aeven is going to be furious," she warned, as she straightened her dress and brushed invisible dirt off of the fabric. She pronounced the name ay-vin, and I was fairly certain she was referring to the Tame King, who the men had called "Aev," pronounced ayv.

"We're sorry, but it couldn't wait," January said, looking at me.

I didn't bother waiting to launch into an explanation. "I found out yesterday that I can see the future. And communicate with Vevol, the goddess. She's been sending me visions of a war that's coming, unless we can figure out a way to stop it. If it comes, it'll be the end of all of us—men and women, seelie and unseelie."

The queen's eyes widened slightly. "Because of us?"

"Because there are twenty of us to hundreds of men, I'd imagine," January said.

Naomi nodded. "The unseelies don't want romantic relationships, but they do want the power boost that comes with having a mate. The girls on my side are unhappy. Most of us would prefer a way back to Earth, or at least the Seelie side of the world. Myself included."

"Ours don't want to leave," January admitted.

She was right; Mare, Dots, and Sunny hadn't ever said anything positive about the unseelies, who would be taking them across the border when their five years were up.

"Women leaving the unseelies could cause a war just as easily as anything else. The men are a ticking time bomb right now," I told the other ladies. "We need a way to give all of them an equal opportunity, without favoring either side."

"They're the ones who came up with the five-year rule," Naomi said, shaking her head. "We've been trying to come up with a way out, but there isn't one. They watch us like hawks. And even if they didn't, we have nowhere else to go."

"What about here?" I asked her, looking around the building again. It was empty, but decently large. "What if we all tell them that the women are tired of their games? The unseelie have a king, and the seelie have the Wild Hunt. Why can't we have our own leadership, and make our own decisions?"

"We have no way to build, and there's not enough space here right now," Naomi pointed out. "Having our own leadership may prove useful, but what would be the purpose? Ultimately, it's still us against the men, and there are hardly any of us. We have no bargaining power, other than our bodies. And I already gave mine to Aeven, to satisfy the last deal."

I considered sharing what Vevol had told me, but hesitated.

"I'm pregnant," January said bluntly.

Naomi's face lost all color. "What?"

January added, "Babies have a lot of bargaining power. It could be a girl. There may not be many of us, but women can create life. We're fucking powerful."

My mind returned to the women hidden away. "We might have more power than we realize," I finally said.

January frowned, and Naomi didn't look convinced.

I looked over at Priel, and then Lian. "We need you to give us a few minutes."

Lian growled. "No."

Priel glared at me.

I glowered back for a long moment before turning to the women. "Vevol gave me the location for a group of female fae. They've been hiding since some huge war a long time ago. I don't know how many of them there are, or anything else about them, but I know where to find them. If we use that as a bargaining chip, we could probably get anything we want from the men. A place to live, food, lessons about how to do necessary shit to stay alive on Vevol without being attached to men..."

Both women were stunned to silence.

The men were, too, though they'd mostly been letting us figure our shit out anyway.

Priel's grip on my waist tightened.

"There could be enough of them to even the odds," Naomi finally said, her eyes bright and hopeful. "Pair that with the possibility of couples who are actually mated being able to have children... we'll have them by the balls."

"I like the way you think," January murmured to her, her own eyes still full of shock.

She hadn't been in Vevol as long as the rest of us. She hadn't seen the fae men truly desperate, and she hadn't seen the way some of the girls despised them or the land.

While she understood the male fae, she was still too new to really understand the ex-human women.

The tears in Naomi's eyes told me that maybe I was too new for that too.

"I'm going to have to call Aeven here," she told us, wiping carefully at her slightly-watery eyes. "I'll give him our offer. I already know what the other girls will say; they'll want to know how soon we can leave. If you don't want to be here when he is, I understand."

"We've got your back," January said easily. She didn't let go of Lian's hand, but I didn't really think he'd let her. The guy seemed pretty damn paranoid, and he had a right to be, considering his lady was pregnant with the first fae baby in who-knows-how-long.

"We can't be here when you talk to him," Priel told the other girls, his voice low and growly. "If the unseelie have a chance to take North before she and I are fully mated, they'll act on it in a heartbeat. Her magic is too powerful for them not to."

The other girls looked at him in surprise.

They didn't understand brands, I assumed, or the importance the fae seemed to place on them.

"He speaks the truth," Lian added. "Branded fae are known to be the most connected to Vevol, and North is undeniably one of them."

I bit back a snort.

Yeah, there definitely wasn't any denying to be had.

"You should hide out in the forest, then," January suggested. "We can come and find you after we talk to Aeven."

"No, they'll need to be farther away. If the unseelie have a chance at getting out of this agreement, they'll do whatever they have to in order to take advantage of it," Naomi said quickly. "Is there a place you can go that only your most trusted friends know about?" She spoke to Priel, and something within me sort of clenched.

If that was jealousy, it could take a hike. This chick was clearly married to an absolute asshole, with no way out of the relationship. There wasn't a chance in hell that she'd be interested in my hound; the girl was probably done with men altogether.

"There is." Priel looked at Lian.

Lian dipped his head. "We'll come find you when the deal has been made and the unseelies have fulfilled their side of whatever bargain we strike."

"Thank you." Priel's fingers pressed lightly against my hip as he began turning me around.

"Even if you decide to mate early, wait until you hear from us," Naomi added. "You're the only one who has the information they'll need, so our control over them extends only as far as your silence. We'll need to get this place built and everyone moved in before we give them what they want."

"We will." I promised her.

She flashed me a small, hopeful smile. "This means more to us than I can say."

I wasn't doing it for her, I thought, but didn't vocalize it.

Instead I just nodded lightly, and let Priel lead me out of the building.

The snow melted beneath our feet as we walked into the heavy silence of the snow-crusted forest around us. I knew that as soon as we made it out of neutral territory, the snow would end. Aeven was the only reason the snow existed there, according to Priel. It was the Tame King's way of separating unseelie land from seelie.

"So, where are we going?" I asked him, my voice soft but my body tense.

I was still worried that he would change his mind about wanting to be with me now that he knew there were actual female fae out there somewhere. What if he found the person whose scent made him positive she belonged to him, like January's had with Lian?

"It's a surprise." He flashed me one of his grins, and my shoulders relaxed slightly.

He still seemed like his normal self, so that was good.

"You're not worried after that conversation?" I asked him, as his hand slid around my hip.

"Why would I be? By the time they get all of that shit figured out, I'll have convinced you to be mine permanently, and probably claimed your skin with my ink as well," he teased.

I raised an eyebrow toward him. "That confident in your ability to win me over, huh?"

"Extremely," he confirmed, squeezing my hip lightly. "I saw it on the walls of your bedroom, Polaris. You'll be mine."

My face heated, but I didn't deny his claim.

He was right; Vevol had showed me that, hadn't she?

"What should we do if I still dream about war after they move the women?" I asked him, still holding his arm as we walked. The snow disappeared, leaving our toes crunching and our flames sizzling over dirt.

"We'll worry about that if we get there. No point in fearing a future that may never greet us."

"I wish my brain would get on board with that," I mumbled.

And I was fairly confident that everyone on Earth or Vevol with any amount of anxiety would feel the same way.

"You'll settle into life here," he promised me. "It'll be easier when most of the world isn't chasing you, trying to convince you to be theirs."

I hoped he was right.

WE SHIFTED, and then ran for the rest of the day. When we finally stumbled into the cave Priel had led me to, which was deep in the mountains, I was ready to drop.

"Why do you like caves so much?" I asked him as I shifted back, my body trembling a little after so many hours of exertion. His arms wrapped around me, and he steadied me as we ducked under a low-hanging rock, pivoting through a crevice I didn't like the looks of.

"I can feel the flames running beneath Vevol while underground. Other fae feel the same way though; the only ones who don't prefer caves are the phoenixes and basilisks, all of which live in the trees. Though, I doubt January will ever make her home in a tree."

"Probably not," I mumbled, pressing my forehead to his neck as he pulled me in close and lifted me off my feet to maneuver me through another crack in the stone.

"This is a cave that only myself and the rest of the Wild Hunt know the location of," he told me, lowering his voice slightly. "We have a few locations like this, hidden away from the others. My pack is probably furious with me after everything that's happened, especially considering that they were already acting strange before we ran back to the Stronghold together. We can't go near them again until things have calmed down a bit."

"That won't be hard. I'm pretty sure Clevv hates me now, and maybe you too. One of the guys who grabbed me outside the stronghold mentioned his name. I think he might've been working with them."

Priel growled at me. "If he's the reason they came after you, I'll kill him."

"I walked out with my brands on display, and he's practically your brother," I reminded him. "You don't need to—ohhh." A happy sigh escaped me as he set me down on a thick, cushy mattress. "Damn."

"The room is fireproof, as is the bed. I'll find you something to eat; you get comfortable." His lips brushed my forehead, but I wrapped my arms around his neck before he could abandon me.

"Wait. If we're going to complete the mate bond, I'll need some kind of plant that interferes with fertility. I'm not ready to have a kid any time soon."

He nodded. "I'll teach you how to tap into your magic and find it yourself."

My eyes widened. "Thank you."

His lips brushed my forehead. "You are very welcome, Gorgeous."

My cheeks were warm with the genuine-feeling compliment,
but I fell asleep as he slipped back out of the cave.

A FEW DAYS passed by quickly, filled with both terrible
dreams and fun, steamy moments with Priel. We played around
a bit, and talked a lot, getting pretty damn hot and heavy both
physically and emotionally, but never taking the plunge into
actual matehood.

Priel always waited until I was going to sleep to slip out of the
cave to find food. He did so again on the fourth night, but the
moment I closed my eyes, I was pulled into a new dream.

Or, I supposed, a vision.

MARE'S SCREAM cut me to the soul.

*My eyes opened, and my arms flew out at my sides as I stumbled.
I caught my balance on a wall—one inside the Stronghold.*

*The door was off its hinges, the massive thing stuck diagonally in
the hallway just in front of the doorway. Beyond it, I saw flashes
of fae fighting. A massive basilisk and sabertooth seemed to be
battling alongside a group of others, holding a wave of men and
creatures at bay.*

*Inside the Stronghold, two thick fae that I recognized held a
bleeding, furious Ervo, who was cuffed at the wrists and ankles in
some kind of thick, stone restraints.*

Another one held Mare, his sharp claws shifted and pressed to the center of her chest. Two more had Sunny and Dots, though both of the other women were draped over their shoulders, unconscious.

Horror clutched my stomach.

They wouldn't hurt us, right?

That was the whole damn deal. They brought us to Vevol, and they didn't hurt us. They couldn't.

Could they?

"Give us the location of the oracle or your chosen female will bleed," the man with the claws snarled at Ervo.

When I recognized him as Clevv, nausea made me sway and clutch the wall.

I had kissed that man.

He had touched my skin.

And now, he was threatening the closest thing I'd ever had to friends.

My eyes jerked back to the other men.

All of them were other members of Priel's pack.

They looked almost as horrified by Clevv's threats as I felt, but said and did nothing to stop him.

My heart dropped into my stomach.

I wasn't built to witness horrors. I wasn't strong enough to see terrible things happen, or watch people hurt. That was a huge

*part of the reason I knew I couldn't live like my parents
did, and—*

*Clevv slashed his fingers over Mare's chest, and her next scream
made my eyes water.*

*Ervo fought his restraints, roaring and wrestling with the men
who held him back, but it was no use.*

He was trapped.

*Clevv lifted his hands to Mare's face, and my whole damn body
quivered in shock as he threatened my friend's eyes.*

*I wanted to scream at him to tell them. To shout that I'd survive
whatever they did to me—that I would rather have them hunting
me down then hurting anyone.*

But the words didn't come out.

I wasn't good under pressure—not like other people were.

And even if they had, it wouldn't have done any good.

I wasn't actually there, no matter what it felt like in the moment.

*"Let the women go and I'll give you what you want," Ervo finally
snarled. "I'll take you there myself."*

*Relief coursed through me as the claws lowered away from
Mare's eyes.*

*"We'll bring this one with us," Clevv growled at the other men, as
he shoved Mare toward Ervo.*

*She crashed into him, her arms wrapping around him and
holding on fiercely. His furious gaze remained fixed on Clevv as*

his head pressed lightly against the side of Mare's, his hands and feet still bound.

"Run the other two to opposite sides of the land until you've convinced them to mate with you. The basilisk and sabertooth will chase you until you've claimed the females," he growled at the men who were holding Sunny and Dots.

They jerked their heads in nods before turning and jogging out of the secret exit.

The same secret exit Priel and I had used.

Had we alerted them to it somehow? Had I triggered it by kissing Clevv?

It didn't sound like the men planned on hurting Sunny and Dots, thankfully, but how long would that last?

"Pick them up," Clevv snarled at the other men, tossing a hand toward Ervo and Mare. The hellhounds beside the phoenix exchanged uncertain expressions, but did as he'd ordered. One of them threw Ervo over his shoulder, despite the massive size and weight of the phoenix. The other carefully picked up Mare.

"Are you okay?" he asked her in a low voice.

"No," she hissed back.

"There aren't words for a proper apology," the hound began.

Bovay; I recognized him as Bovay.

"Don't even try," Mare snarled, though her voice shook.

Sorrow filled the hellhound's eyes as he followed Clevv and the man holding Ervo out through the back door.

"Where are we going?" Clevv demanded.

"There's a cave in the mountains," Ervo growled back. "It's the first place Priel would've taken her to hide away."

I started to jog after them, to figure out what was going to happen next, but then I felt hands on my waist.

My gaze jerked down to my abdomen, but I didn't see anything.

The world tilted around me suddenly, and then I was ripped back into my body.

TWELVE

I GASPED as I jerked upright, finding myself face to face with Clevv.

My body froze.

Just completely froze.

A shudder rolled down my spine.

"I'm here, pretty one." The hellhound dragged a sharp fingernail down the side of my face.

My mind struggled to put the pieces together.

I hadn't been seeing the future, that time.

It had to have been the past, didn't it?

How was that possible?

"Where's Priel?" My voice wobbled slightly.

Anger flared in the man's eyes. "We have him restrained. I want him dead, but the rest of the pack wants mates."

Mates.

Right.

Priel was the only one who could get the portal open—so they needed him.

Relief nearly had me sagging into the mattress, but I was smart enough to realize that things were still really damn serious.

They still had Mare.

And Ervo.

And Sunny and Dots.

And me.

Things were *not* stacked in our favor.

"He won't force you to do anything, ever again," Clevv practically purred at me. His fingers slid into my hair, his hand cupping the back of my neck.

Instinct told me to argue. To point out that Priel had never forced me to do anything I didn't silently want to do, that he was my future, and that I wanted him.

But the possessiveness in Clevv's gaze kept me quiet.

I wasn't going to encourage him. Not even a little. But arguing would only enrage him, if he really thought I belonged to him. He had already proven he was willing to hurt Mare to find me; there wasn't a chance in hell that I'd be safe with him.

So I kept my mouth shut.

He leaned toward me, as if to kiss me, and I leaned back.

It was time to lie.

"I'm not ready," I said, letting my voice shake like it wanted to.

He stilled.

His eyes softened.

"Of course. You can have all the time you need."

When he stretched a hand out toward me, I slipped mine inside it. There was no way I was getting around that shit, and I was much more willing to hold his hand than let him kiss me.

"What are we doing?" I asked him, hoping he would believe that I considered us a team.

"Going home, of course." He slid his fingers between mine, and I fought the nausea that followed.

We were going to be fine.

I hoped so, at least.

"What about Priel and Ervo?" My voice stayed even.

"We'll have to keep them chained until you and I are mated and Mare has chosen one of my brothers, of course," he said easily.

Of course.

If my stomach wasn't empty, I would've retched.

"There's plenty of space to do so back at home," he promised, like that was supposed to reassure me.

It obviously didn't.

I stayed quiet as he led me the rest of the way out of the cave. He moved through it much more slowly than Priel had, but I would've gone at a snail's pace if it meant he didn't put his hands on me.

We finally made it out of the cave twenty minutes later.

My eyes stung when I surveyed the scene outside the entrance.

Ervo and Priel were on their knees, both men bruised and actively bleeding. Priel was slouched over, clearly unconscious, and Ervo was staring at the man in front of me with so much fury that I wondered if Clevv would combust.

Then again, it wouldn't hurt him even if he did.

We were all creatures of fire, after all.

Mare was wrapped in the arms of one of the other hellhounds. She looked somewhere between furious and terrified, but relief filled her eyes when she saw me.

Neither of us spoke, though.

What was there to say?

We had both been *captured* by an insane asshole who had decided I was going to be his, and that Mare was going to mate with one of the other hounds.

"Get the phoenix in the sky again, with your claws to his throat and to the dragon girl's too," Clevv commanded the hound holding Mare, and the four behind Priel and Ervo.

The man holding Mare bristled, just slightly. I side-eyed Clevv, trying to decide whether or not he had noticed. He hadn't.

Clevv seemed to think he had some sort of power over the rest of them. I wasn't sure where said power was coming from, but there was one thing I was sure about.

The seelie fae *hated* being controlled.

And if I could play along long enough, and maybe nudge the idea that he was acting like he was in charge, then I could probably get the other fae working with him to realize they didn't like him any more than I did.

If I could do *that*, there was a good chance I could get Mare and myself away from them.

And if Mare and I got away, Priel and Ervo would have no reason to play nice.

Then, hell would break loose.

And all of us would be free.

Deciding that was the best possible plan, I averted my eyes and remained silent as Clevv put his arm over my shoulders, watching the men as they wrestled Ervo off the ground. Mare was hauled up onto his back after he shifted to his massive flaming bird form, her body pinned between two other fae men. One of them had his claws to Ervo's throat, and the other gripped Mare tightly.

When they soared into the sky, Clevv barked commands about carrying Priel to the other hounds, then pulled me up onto his back as he shifted.

I despised the feel of his muscles beneath me when he took off running, so I grabbed fistfuls of his fur, hopefully causing him a little pain as he sprinted away with me.

As we left the cave behind, I peered over my shoulder. The man who carried a bound, unconscious Priel, followed behind us.

At least my hound was safe for the time being.

Everything else, we would figure out a way to deal with.

PRIEL WOKE up less than an hour into the long, long run. Clevv stopped running, and Ervo circled above us.

The fae wrestled him, until they all shifted and began tearing into each other.

I couldn't watch that.

"Don't fight them, Priel," I called out.

One of the men's bodies went flying, and then a bleeding, growling Priel in his hound form was glowering at me, but had stopped fighting. The other hound stood a few feet to his side, watching the stronger fae warily. Priel's front paws were still bound together, and his back ones were too, yet he didn't bother looking down.

I could tell he was checking to make sure I was okay, trying to figure out what had happened.

"We're fine. You have to stop fighting," I urged.

He snarled at me, gesturing with his head.

I could imagine what he was furious about.

Me, riding on Clevv's back.

There were bigger issues, but the fae's possessiveness was undeniable and didn't seem to be something they could control.

"If you want Priel to follow you peacefully, I need to shift and run on my own feet," I told Clevv.

Ultimately, the traitorous pack outnumbered me and Priel, so I couldn't just make an executive decision and jump off Clevv's back. Priel and Ervo were among the strongest of the seelies, but it was Priel's shitty family who had us. If anyone could keep up with the Wild Hunt, it was their own damn families.

And besides that, they had already proven they were willing to hurt Mare to get what they wanted.

Clevv growled and snapped his teeth at Priel.

Priel snarled back, and I saw the way my hound's body tensed.

He was going to attack Clevv.

Honestly, I thought Clevv and the other men would be willing to kill Priel if things got too out of hand. And considering that he was still bound, the chance of him surviving if they wanted him dead was minimal.

So I shoved away the paralyzing fear in my chest and lunged between the men.

My feet hit the ground just in time for both of them to halt and snarl at me as I stood between them.

"No one needs to die," I said firmly.

Priel's snapping teeth told me he disagreed.

I didn't know if there was a way out of this situation that didn't include at least one death, so I didn't necessarily think he was wrong.

I just wanted to make sure that death wasn't Priel's.

"I'll run on my own," I told both of them.

Clevv shifted, and I forced my gaze to remain steady despite the rapid pounding of my heart.

"Priel will take koveko or we'll knock him unconscious ourselves, then," Clevv growled at me.

Priel shifted back too, and I fought the urge to step behind him and let him protect me.

He couldn't defend me in this moment; I needed to protect both of us.

"As long as no one touches my female, I'll take the damn poison," Priel said.

My eyes widened. "What?"

Clevv glared at Priel while answering my question. "Koveko is a bulbous plant with a liquid within it that renders its drinker unconscious for half of a day." There was a tense pause. "And this female belongs to me, not you."

Shit.

There was going to be carnage.

"Get the plant. Priel will drink it," I said quickly

The man growled behind me, and I spun to face him. Our eyes locked.

I couldn't say what I wanted to say.

That I needed him to play along until we could figure out a safe way to get ourselves, Mare, and Ervo out of the situation.

So instead I narrowed my eyes at him.

He liked it when I got sassy with him; it proved to him that I was still myself, that I wasn't scared or confused.

He glared back at me, but I saw his eyes soften slightly.

His head jerked in a nod, and I looked back at Clevv.

Clevv barked an order at one of the other hellhounds—who looked irked with the command, but followed it. He disappeared into the forest for a few tense moments.

None of the rest of us moved until he came back, peeled the top off of a fruit that looked like something between an onion and a tulip, and held it to Priel's lips.

My hellhound stared at me as he drank the liquid, not closing his eyes until they rolled back into his head and he collapsed.

His pack members caught him before he hit the ground, and Clevv growled at me that I needed to shift and stay next to him.

My pounding, panicked heart and I shifted anyway, and when Clevv started to run, I followed.

. . .

WE MADE it back to the land I recognized as the pack's space before Priel woke up.

Mare, Ervo, and the hounds with them landed.

The men shifted back, and I did too. I should've stayed in my hound form though; I felt safer when I was a badass flaming-bear-wolf-thing than my wimpy human self.

Yeah, technically I was a fae, but I still *felt* human most of the time.

"North will come home with me," Clevv announced. "Chain Priel and Ervo, and compete to determine who will claim Mare."

Fury had me clenching my fists.

What a bastard.

"We haven't heard the female agree to be yours," one of the men remarked, folding his arms over his chest. His eyes blazed, and excitement coursed through me.

I knew they weren't happy with him acting as their leader.

Clevv scoffed. "She already kissed me. The oracle is mine."

"She did a lot more than just *kiss* Priel, yet he doesn't get to claim her without her permission," Mare pointed out.

Clevv growled, but murmurs of agreement rolled through the rest of the group.

"You hurt the dragon female. That wasn't part of the agreement," Bovay pointed out.

Clevv grabbed me by the biceps. I froze in place, trying not to show the bastard that I was terrified as his nails dug into my arms, shifting into claws. "I did what I had to do to claim the woman who was meant to be mine."

"You said Priel was forcing her," one of the men argued.

"He *was*. You all saw him," Clevv snarled. "She wanted *me*."

The hellhounds who had been following his orders exchanged uncertain looks.

Clevv's gaze jerked around the group.

He seemed to realize that shit was about to stop working in his favor—and he acted.

My face crashed into his back as he threw me over his shoulder and spun around, sprinting across the land. We passed half a dozen holes in the ground in what felt like the blink of an eye, and then we were plummeting.

His feet met the floor, and then my *ass* met it too. My palms smacked the stone as I held on, trying to keep myself upright.

He was shutting something over the entrance to his cave a moment later, closing us in. I watched in horror as he welded the metal door shut with his palms, and then quickly covered it with two more layers of something that had already been propped against the wall, apparently prepared to block the door.

His eyes were wild and desperate when he looked at me.

I fought the urge to curl up in a ball and hide.

"Are you going to attack me?" I asked him instead, forcing myself to feign confidence that I absolutely did not feel.

He seemed to deflate a little. "Of course not."

The fact that he still thought that was a given after injuring my friend spoke volumes about the mental stability he *didn't* possess.

He added, "We all saw how Priel forced you away from me. He didn't accept that you'd chosen me."

"I chose you as a *temporary mate*," I said, my voice harsher than it should've been given the perilous situation. "I told you I wasn't looking for anything serious, and you said you were fine with that."

His eyes darkened. "I said you would be my future mate. When I saw your brands, I knew for sure that we'd be far more than temporary. Vevol made you for me."

I choked on a horrified laugh.

Vevol hadn't *made me*. She had changed me, sure, but I was born on Earth.

And the fact that he hadn't decided he wanted things to be permanent with me until he realized how many brands I had was another strike against him.

"I never agreed to that," I said, looking away from the man and letting my gaze linger on the wall in front of me.

"Fate decided." His voice was low.

Apparently he now thought of himself as fate. Whatever the hell that meant in the scheme of things where Vevol was both the world and the goddess, I didn't know.

So I said nothing.

"I need to feed you," he mumbled to himself, raking a hand through his hair as he strode toward the small, fae-style kitchen on the other side of the room.

There wasn't anywhere to sit other than his bed, since his home was shaped the same as Priel's. I wasn't going anywhere near the damned bed, so I scooted the two feet between myself and the wall, then turned my back to the stone. Sitting up like that, I could see the entirety of the cave and was ready for an attack.

He started cooking, and I carefully watched the spices he put into the food. I knew there was at least one questionable spice in Vevol, but where there was one, there were usually more. The one I knew about, the men had said made your parts swell and tingle a bit, and would lead to hours of pleasure.

With the right partner, that sounded crazy hot. I'd seen the future version of Priel use it on the future version of me enough times to be hella turned-on when I thought about it outside of Clevv's cave.

But as far as food went, I didn't know what that spice would look like or taste like if it was put inside something. So, knowing that it existed made me extremely reluctant to touch any food that Clevv was making.

He hadn't had a problem hurting Mare, so why would he have a problem with drugging me to get his way?

My eyes flicked to the divider over the entrance to the cave, and I let myself hope that Priel was waking up and would be breaking in and rescuing my ass in the near future.

Because if he didn't, something told me I might end up with another set of scars to match the ones I earned the last time I had to escape from some bastard who thought he could do whatever the hell he wanted to me.

Thirteen
Priel

A wave of ice-cold water jerked me out of sleep.

"What the hell?" I growled, rubbing at my eyes with the back of my arm as my fire burned away the chill immediately.

"Your female has been taken, brother," Ervo's low voice had my body going still.

My mind returned to the forest.

The betrayal of the pack I had considered my family.

Clevv's hands on North's skin.

His insistence that she was his.

Her, asking me to drink the poison.

I was on my feet a heartbeat later, snarling and looking around the area.

We had returned to the pack's land, apparently.

Mare and Ervo stood near me, with a large bucket that I assumed had held ice-water a minute earlier sitting on the ground between them.

My packmates were in a small group off to the side.

I wanted their heads removed from their bodies.

But I had bigger shit to worry about, and I didn't know if any of them had actually done anything that deserved dying over.

I glowered at Bovay, knowing he would answer even if I was a risk to his life. "Where the fuck is Clevv?"

"He took North into his cave, and blocked off the entrance."

Curses spewed from me.

I started to pace.

We all wanted the privacy that came with being able to close ourselves into our homes. We'd designed our caves to be impenetrable when we wanted them to be.

With enough time and effort, I could get through the metal and stone door of sorts. I was confident in that.

But how long did I have before he touched her again?

Hurt her?

Tried to force her to mate with him?

A roar escaped me, and I fought hard to think through the fear pounding in my head.

"If he hears us trying to get in, he'll do something drastic," Ervo said in a low voice. "I think we're going to have to wait him out."

"She dreams of the future every night," I snarled back. "Of us, together. Or of the war. She can't sleep in there with him."

Mare's voice was gentle when she replied, "I don't think she has a choice."

Bovay walked up to me, Ervo, and Mare, his expression hesitant.

That hesitance was a good call, because as soon as my female was in my arms, we'd be fighting to his death.

"Clevv eats with us every night. He won't have enough food with him to last them more than two or three days," Bovay said in a low voice. "Eventually, she'll get hungry, and the instincts to feed and care for his mate will force him to emerge. When he—"

"She's not his fucking mate," I roared back, white-hot anger pumping through my veins as I grabbed the bastard by the throat. "North belongs to me, of her own free will. I gave everyone the chance I was obligated to give, and the whole damn time, she dreamed of our future together. If Clevv so much as pulls one hair from her head, I'll make your death so long and painful that you'll beg Vevol to end your life with every excruciating thought that crosses your mind."

He didn't flinch or shrink away.

Just stared at me as I glowered at him.

Finally, I dropped my hold on his throat and stepped back.

I started pacing again.

Bovay walked back to the group of traitors.

If they were wise, they would've taken the opportunity to put as much distance between us as was possible.

"You need to eat something," Mare said to Ervo. "We were flying for a long time." She looked at me. "You do too, Priel."

"My mate is locked in a cave with a man who thinks she belongs to him. I'm not *hungry*," I snarled back.

"Brother." Ervo's cold gaze was furious. Not many people knew him well enough to read his emotions, but I was one of them. "Don't speak to her that way."

I glowered back at him, but jerked my head in a nod.

He wouldn't get an apology.

Mare wouldn't, either.

They were the ones who had shown Clevv the location of the cave. They were at least a part of the reason she was down there. And though there was likely a reasonable explanation for that, I wasn't interested in hearing it.

"I'll show you which plants are edible," Ervo told Mare, his hand touching her lower back lightly as he led her into the forest, in the opposite direction of my packmates.

I halted when the answer to my problem hit me in the fucking chest.

Her name.

I had her name.

Pride and relief swelled within me.

"Polaris, I need you in my arms," I growled into the air, body tensing and preparing for a fight.

The space in front of me shimmered, and then North was on her ass in that space, falling backward as if whatever she'd been leaning against had up and vanished.

I was on my knees, holding her upright, in a heartbeat.

She stared at me in shock for a few moments.

And then, she threw her arms around me.

Her grip was hard and desperate.

Her body was soft, and shaking.

But she was there.

And she was safe.

"You're okay?" she demanded, leaning away from me and looking me up and down.

"No. But you're here, and that's what matters." I cupped her face, pressing my forehead to hers. She clung to me, the shaking in her body only seeming to grow more pronounced.

"We need to seal the mating bond. This can't happen again," North whispered, her voice quivering as much as she was.

"After I've ended Clevv's life," I agreed, standing up. I hauled her into my arms as I did so, and she buried her face against my neck.

"I can't believe I forgot about using your name," she whispered.

"It's been a long few days." I stroked her back lightly, cradling her like the precious, fragile thing she was. "And I prefer you not having to see me tear the head off of a man you kissed at one point."

She shuddered, and I held her tighter.

"Mare and Ervo went to get food; they'll be back soon. You'll feel a little better with something in your belly."

She made a noise of agreement that didn't sound anywhere near certain, but I continued rubbing her back and holding her to me.

I had no plans to let go of her until Clevv came out of that hole.

The deaths of the traitors could wait.

All of the fighting could wait.

Because my female was safe in my arms, and no one else would ever touch her again.

FOURTEEN
NORTH

PRIEL HAD BEEN growly and possessive before the abduction, but after? I wasn't sure he was completely sane. He carried my exhausted butt around until he had to put me down so I could eat. Even then, he really didn't want to let go of me, but I didn't think he could physically sit still for long enough to hold me while I ate.

So I sat down and went to town on the delicious fresh fruit and vegetables Mare and Ervo had found—which Priel refused to do—and my hound paced.

There were flames blazing in his eyes, and while I knew that didn't mean he was crazy or anything, it did mean that his emotions were sort of feral.

For the most part, I seemed to be into feral. But now, it had crossed into unhealthy territory.

Yes, I knew that Priel needed to confront Clevv.

They would fight.

Clevv was willing to hurt women, so he would most-likely die.

I was okay with that.

Hence my patience as I sat down next to Mare, eating.

She looked just as exhausted as I felt.

"You should get some sleep," I murmured to her.

"I can't," she admitted, then bit her lip.

I waited.

She remained silent, but her expression grew sort of haunted. Eventually, she whispered, "He attacked me. Clevv. I thought we were safe here, but we're not. Ana was right."

Though I was out of practice when it came to talking to people —and relating with them especially—my mom had always taken my hand or pulled me in for a hug when I was struggling with something.

I wrapped my arm around Mare's back, pulling her closer. Her arm wrapped around mine too, and we scooted closer together until we were sort of snuggling.

"This was my fault," I admitted softly. "He thought I was his because I kissed him. The rest of the pack thought Priel was forcing me to be with him because he got possessive after I kissed Clevv, so they thought they were doing the right thing. There are no excuses for Clevv; he lost his mind. But he didn't lose it without cause. I should've made sure he knew that I didn't like it when he touched me, and that I was choosing to stay with Priel."

"But shit like this wouldn't happen with the unseelie." Mare's eyes were unfocused. "The rules and the coldness... it's a protection."

"I'm sure it can be. But distancing yourself from everyone the way that they do only causes pain. I think I know that better than anyone," I said quietly.

She looked over at me, her eyes a little watery. "No one ever physically hurt me on Earth."

"Then you should count yourself lucky." I gave her a tiny smile, turning to look out in front of me.

Priel was still pacing, but when I caught a glimpse of the side of his face, I realized he was listening to our conversation.

Ervo probably was too, I thought, as I glanced over at him. He sat sprawled across the ground, his gaze focused intensely on Mare.

The way he looked at her was almost enough to give *me* the tingles.

There was shuffling and growling off to our left, and when Mare and I looked over, we found Priel and Ervo standing between us and the group of hellhounds that Priel used to consider his pack.

"Any closer to her and you forfeit your lives." Ervo's calm threat didn't scare me, but I also didn't doubt for a second that he would follow through with it.

"She deserves an apology," one of the fae growled back. "And a knife in her hand."

A knife?

In her hand?

I looked at Mare, but she looked just as lost as me.

"We should've stopped Clevv," another of the hellhounds said to Ervo gravely. "We were taken by surprise when he acted the way he did, and didn't respond correctly. Your female deserves to end us herself."

Mare's eyes flooded with horror.

I knew her well enough to be sure that she wasn't going to kill anyone.

"She does," Ervo agreed.

All of the men looked at us.

Mare's face went ashy, and she gripped my arm tightly.

I spoke up for her. "Mare hasn't decided what consequences she wants to enforce yet. When she does, she'll let you know."

The men waited a long moment before they split up. The traitors went back to the place they'd been gathered a few minutes earlier, while Priel and Ervo returned to their previous positions even more intense-like than they had before.

"You're good at that," Mare murmured to me. "Not letting people walk all over you."

I laughed humorlessly. "For this ten minutes. As soon as shit goes down, I freeze up. Probably because of my past."

"What happened to you?" she asked. "You had so many scars.

My throat swelled, but I admitted, "My parents were very overprotective, so I didn't get out much. They arranged a marriage for me, but we were betrayed. I was in the car, and the bastard I was supposed to marry told me he was going to kill me and make a statement out of it. He was so proud."

I shook my head a little. "There were two options. Accept my fate, or jump out of the vehicle. They thought I was a scared little mouse, so they hadn't bothered barring the doors or anything. I jumped. And then I survived in the forest, until my dad's people finally found me. Spent a long time in the hospital, afterward. Nothing they could do about the scars."

The horror had returned to Mare's eyes. "I'm so sorry."

"You don't need to apologize for something you had nothing to do with." I looked away from her, staring out at the scenery again. Vevol was so beautiful, with its strange trees and rocky, rough mountains.

"Still. That's just... damn. We knew you were strong, but that's next level."

"If you were in the situation, you would've done the same thing."

"I don't know if I would've," she admitted.

"Then you need to believe in yourself more. You're stronger than you realize. If you can't sleep now, focus on getting even stronger so that if something like this ever happens again, you can protect yourself. You're a damn *dragon*, Mare."

She was silent for a few minutes before she finally said, "I need to learn how to shift."

"You do," I agreed. "Calian probably knows a dragon or two who could teach you."

She sighed heavily. "I hope so."

It was time to change the subject.

"Did I tell you about the meeting with Naomi?" I asked her.

When she said I had not, we spent the next hour discussing how things would change when we created our own neutral land, never bringing up the fae women we would need to retrieve to make that happen.

By the time that hour wound down, Mare looked so exhausted that I didn't think she'd remain upright for much longer.

When Ervo asked, Priel pointed him toward one of the community caves, so Mare could sleep while he watched over and protected her.

She didn't argue, following him to the cave after giving me a quick hug.

TIME PASSED and Priel continued pacing, shooting glares at the group of hellhounds every few minutes even though they had yet to try pushing the boundaries again.

I started to wonder if Clevv was ever going to come out.

The man was at least a little insane, but that didn't tell me what would happen when he emerged. If anything, it made me less certain about whatever he was going to do next.

My yawns began, and over time, grew longer and larger.

When I curled up on the ground, Priel snapped his teeth and scooped me up.

He hauled me over to the cave where Ervo was watching out for Mare, and called into the opening, "I need you to take a turn on watch."

There was a long pause, and then Ervo came climbing out with a snoring Mare draped over his shoulder and one of the massive beanbag things clenched tightly in his fist. It dragged behind him a bit because of its size, but his gigantic muscles didn't seem to have a problem with that.

"Kill any of them you want," Priel told the phoenix, adjusting his grip on me. My head pressed to his chest, and he rubbed my back lightly. "I'll listen for Clevv."

I shouldn't have felt safe while he was telling his buddy to murder people and talking about the person he was going to kill, but I did.

Maybe I belonged in the mafia more than I'd thought.

Priel held me carefully as he jogged to his home, and jumped inside so smoothly that I barely felt the motion at all.

Those had to be some massive thighs.

I should probably study them, to see just how massive.

With my hands, if I wanted to be more thorough.

My lips curved upward slightly at the thought.

He lowered me to the bed and brushed hair out of my eyes. His lips brushed my forehead, and cheek, and throat, before he straightened and stepped away.

Something within me said he was going to start pacing again if I didn't convince him to get under the blankets with me.

"Will you hold me while I sleep?" I asked him, scooting over to make space.

"No." His voice was gruff.

I frowned. "Why not?"

His expression hardened. "You smell like Clevv."

Oh.

I hadn't considered that.

"Then why did you put me in your bed? It's going to smell like Clevv too, now." I slid out from beneath the blankets, putting a hand on the wall to help me stand on my wobbly, exhausted feet.

"We're not coming back here, so it doesn't matter." His gaze dared me to argue.

I glared back at him. "Stop talking to me like I'm the enemy. I didn't know he was coming after us until right before I woke up with him hovering over me. And obviously, I didn't know that he was going to get this attached when I kissed him, or I wouldn't have even considered it. He said he was okay with me using him just so I wouldn't get hit on by the other guys. The relationship was supposed to be fake."

"Fae don't do fake relationships, North. Look at us." He tossed a hand toward me.

"We're different. I've seen Nev and Dots together, and Sunny and Teris. They're just friends. I heard last month that Ervo even told Mare he sees her as a sister."

"They're all full of shit," Priel said, stepping toward me. There were only a few inches between our chests, and the only fabric separating our skin was that of my fireproof tank top. Both of our chests rose and fell rapidly, the anger and exhaustion functioning as one to get us both worked up over this silly argument. "Every one of them. We're selfish bastards, Gorgeous."

He studied me for a long moment.

My mouth was dry as I struggled with my thoughts.

What was he saying?

Was he suggesting that the arrangement between us and the Wild Hunt had been a setup?

His voice was low and rough. "You can't really think we offered ourselves up out of the goodness of our hearts. If becoming mates over time was possible, and there were only five female candidates, you'd better believe that we manipulated those cards perfectly. You see us as innocent because we're virgins, but that doesn't make us stupid."

My throat swelled. "Did you rig the name-drawing?"

He scoffed. "Of course we rigged the damn drawing. I wasn't going to end up mated to Dots. Have you seen how much she smiles?"

I couldn't suppress the snort that escaped me.

"Sunny was into you," I threw out.

"Sunny was attracted to my body. I wanted a woman whose soul would speak to me."

I crossed my arms over my chest. "And you think that's me?"

"I think the way you hide your sadness with anger touches my fucking heart."

His blunt words made me inhale sharply.

"And I think the way you keep your thoughts private until you're ready to share them has wrapped itself around my filthy, ink-stained soul." He covered the distance between us and wrapped his hands around my face, tilting my head back until our eyes met. "I didn't want one of the playful females. I wanted the intense one who snarls at other bastards when they get too close. I wanted the woman with paint beneath her fingernails and crusted in her hair. The one who studied me when she thought I wasn't looking, and hid paintings of my ink within her own art."

"You didn't know all of those things when we did the name drawing," I countered.

"I didn't need to."

He lowered his face and slowly brushed his lips over mine. Mine responded, but he pulled away before I could intensify the kiss. "Having Clevv's scent on your skin is making it extremely difficult to suppress the urge to throw you against the wall and fuck you, Polaris. I need you to get in the shower, now. Just burning away his touch isn't enough; I want to scrub it from your skin."

I extracted my hands from his. "I never said I wasn't in favor of having sex against a wall."

He caught my arm, his eyes narrowing. "How many times have you had sex that way?"

A snort escaped me.

Easy answer.

"None."

His eyes heated. "How many times have you had sex, period?"

Well, now we were moving into dangerous territory.

I wasn't sure how he'd react when he found out I was a virgin too.

Proud?

Worried?

Excited?

Even more possessive?

Really damn ready to have sex?

I didn't know.

But I did know that I wouldn't have his full attention until Clevv wasn't a threat anymore, so I wasn't about to proposition him. No way in hell was our first time going to be while he was listening for sounds that might mean my abductor was coming out of his hidey-hole.

"We're not having this conversation right now," I told him, stepping out of his grip and striding toward the bathroom.

"It's that bad?" he growled, fury lining his voice.

I scoffed, turning on the shower.

Even if I had been with a bunch of guys, it shouldn't matter to him. That was then, and this was now. My past was in my past, regardless of what I'd done back on Earth.

Then again, when the fae got possessive about that shit, they got *really* possessive about it.

"I need the number, North."

I stripped my tank over my head, ignoring his warning.

"Polaris," he growled at me.

I pushed my shorts down and stepped out of them, and then into the shower.

He followed me, though his shorts remained on.

I reached for the soap.

His hand caught my wrist, pinning it and the rest of my back to the shower's wall.

His flames burned over both of us, and he slid his hand between my thighs.

I sucked in a breath as he grabbed my core, the base of his gigantic hand pressing into my clit while his fingers found both of my entrances.

If I wasn't into all that rough shit, I probably would've been shocked or uncomfortable.

As it was, I was dripping wet. And not just where the water had hit me.

I lifted my hand that wasn't pinned to the wall up to his shoulder, needing something to hold on to.

"You belong to me," he said, his voice low and feral. "Give me the number."

"Tell me why you want to know," I countered breathlessly.

"So I can learn exactly how many times I need to fuck you to erase their memories from your mind."

Yeah, his snarl only made me hotter.

"You aren't very good at bartering," I told him. "You're desperate; I could ask you for anything I want right now, and I bet you would give it to me."

"You can be damn sure I would."

His thick fingers teased my entrances, and I breathed in sharply.

"You want to make this a trade? Fine. Give me the number, and I'll get you off. Don't give it to me, and I'll make you so wet that you beg me, before walking away."

"That's just mean."

"I never claimed to be nice." He slid the tip of his fingers into me, rocking the base of his palm against my clit slowly.

My heart pounded so loudly it was difficult to think.

The pressure of his touches made me pant.

He slid his fingers further inside me, and I clenched around him as I neared the edge.

The bastard wouldn't really stop me, would he? He—

Ohh, shit.

I cried out, so damn close to the edge.

But his hand stilled, right then.

I groaned, but he pinned me in place with his hips when I tried to rock them.

"The number, Polaris?" His growl only made me more needy.

The bastard had played me like a damn fiddle, and I wasn't even mad about it.

"None," I growled back.

Silence surrounded us as our eyes remained locked together. I could see the shock in his, and my toes curled as I watched it transform to hot, possessive need.

And slowly, he resumed the motions of his hand.

My knees knocked together as the pleasure swelled within me.

My nails dug into his shoulder and back as I lost control with a cry, and he growled his approval when the scent of his blood met my nose.

"I made you bleed," I panted, still rocking my hips lightly.

"If you knew how hard that makes me, you'd keep those sexy little claws to yourself," he grumbled back, not removing his fingers from inside me.

"Why? You heal fast."

"That's fucking right. I like the pain."

"I know you do. Oracle, remember?" I flashed him a smirk, and his eyes heated.

His grip on my core and hip tightened. "What are you going to do to me in our future, Gorgeous?"

I lifted a shoulder. "You'll just have to wait and see."

When I eased his hand out from between my thighs, he let me step away and grab the oddly-shaped soap. Before I could drag it over my body, he plucked it from my fingers and spun me around so my back was to him.

His hands moved slowly and thoroughly over my skin as he cleaned me. My eyes shut, and I let myself enjoy the moment.

His breath was in my ear a moment later. "As soon as I've dealt with Clevv, I'm taking you home and stripping you naked. You won't be leaving our place again until I've claimed every inch of this gorgeous, delicious body. Understand?"

"You are so damn bossy," I mumbled back.

"Always." He growled the agreement. "Get used to it. You won't be complaining when I'm ordering you to shatter on my cock. Any other time, we can argue all you want."

The bastard had me with that one.

"I thought this was your house," I told him, changing the subject before things got too sexually charged again. "I've never dreamed about it before, though."

"This was my home with the pack. They lost my trust—and will probably lose their lives too. Now, you're my pack. Along with the rest of the Wild Hunt, I suppose. I have another place hidden away, closer to my brothers' mountains. There are lakes all over the place, and many different kinds of plants. It's beautiful; you'll like it."

His soapy hands dragged down my thighs, ignoring my core for the time being. I was pretty damn confident he'd clean that too, though.

"I hope so," I admitted.

His lips brushed my forehead. "I'm sorry I didn't protect you from Clevv. The bastards snuck up on me, but even if I'd known they were coming, I wouldn't have expected them to do what they did."

"No one suspects betrayal from the people they love. I don't blame you for their choices." My eyes closed as his lips brushed my temple too.

"I still feel shitty about it, though," he admitted.

"Get over it."

He chuckled, and my lips curved upward.

My smile faded as I remembered the way Ervo had looked at Mare, though. And all of the shit that had gone down in my dream. "I know you're furious with Clevv and the rest of the pack, and you have every right to be. But I don't think anything the pack did to either of us is bad enough that they should die, Priel. Death is permanent. They could turn their shit around and become better after this."

The man's hands returned to my abdomen and breasts, slowly scrubbing my skin. "What are you asking me, Gorgeous?" There was an edge to his voice that I didn't particularly like, but this was a sensitive subject, so it didn't surprise me.

"I'm asking you to leave them alive."

There was a long, long pause.

Trying to voice things in a violent fae's perspective, I added, "Clevv abducted me, but that was partially my fault for leading him on. He didn't physically hurt me. I saw what he did to Mare, though, and Ervo was forced to watch every second of it. They held him down while Clevv hurt her. If he's really as devoted to her as you think he is, then doesn't he deserve to kill Clevv, and the traitors too if that's what he wants? Isn't what they did to Ervo's mate worse than what he did to me?"

Priel's fingers dug lightly into my belly, and my abdomen tightened at the ticklish feel of it. "You're trying to talk sense into me now, female?" he growled at me, his voice sounding tired.

The man had to be at least as exhausted as I was.

"I'm just being a good mate," I said innocently.

He gave me a gruff chuckle, and buried his face against my neck. Even with the water dulling his senses, I was certain he could still smell me, because I could still smell him. And as always, he smelled incredible.

"I'll think about it," he mumbled against my neck. "For now, just be with me."

My heart swelled.

Turning in his arms so our chests met, I went up on my tiptoes and pressed my lips to his.

He lifted me up off the ground and into his arms easily, positioning the length of his erection against my clit as he parted my lips with his tongue.

Our mouths made love as I rocked my hips, dragging him against me in a way that made me shudder. When I stopped moving, his hands on my thighs did the work for me.

I arched against him as I cried into his mouth, the orgasm tearing through me.

The motion lined the head of his cock up with my entrance, his tip pressing into me slightly, and we both inhaled sharply.

My wild eyes met his. "I want you."

His jaw clenched, but he said nothing.

"Clevv could be out any minute, and I need to find the plants that stop fertility before we go further," I said, even though what I wanted to do was slide down his erection. My breathing was already so damn fast I might as well have been jogging.

Veins in his neck and forehead bulged so much they threatened to pop through the skin.

"We can't yet," I told him, even though it hurt to do so.

He finally jerked his head in the sharpest, tiniest nod, and set me down on my feet slowly.

I felt the loss as soon as he pulled out of me.

My body clenched at the idea of having him filling me soon.

What would it be like?

He peeled a chunk of wet hair off my cheek, and it felt like he electrocuted me when his skin brushed mine.

I jumped back a little, and his eyes widened before the biggest grin stretched his cheeks.

"What was that?" I asked.

"The mate bond." His eyes were bright and excited. "Do you feel your body relaxing, and your energy returning?"

Now that he'd mentioned it, I did. Even the slight hunger I'd felt was fading.

"The magic will keep us both healthier and stronger." He tilted my head back and kissed me, then growled against my mouth, "Fuck, I can't wait for this thing to settle. For you to be mine, permanently."

"Me too," I whispered, reaching between us and wrapping my fingers around his cock.

His whole body flexed, and he groaned as I started to stroke him slowly.

"Let me take care of you now, and then we can get some sleep or go back to waiting for Clevv."

He growled fiercely. "Don't talk about that bastard while you're touching me."

I grinned. "What are you going to do to me if I refuse?"

"Maybe I'll put you on your knees and feed my cock between those sexy little lips." His grip on my face tightened.

"Don't tempt me." I dragged my tongue over his nipple, and his whole body shuddered as he roared, losing control with that sexy, tight grip on my cheeks.

FIFTEEN

THOUGH THE ELECTRICITY between us had wiped away my exhaustion, Priel still made me get some sleep in his arms before we climbed back out of the cave and rejoined the others. Mare was still sleeping on the bean bag thing, so I climbed up next to her.

She woke up a few hours later, and we chatted as the day went on. Priel and Ervo both sat in front of us, taking up a ton of space on the ground with their gigantic bodies.

After the sexy time we'd spent together in the shower, my hound had finally stopped pacing. That made me feel sort of pleased with myself.

That night and the next day passed similarly, though without any moments of escape, despite the awful war dreams I had every time I slept. I would've tried to hit on Priel, to get him to take me back to his cave, but the man was growing more on-guard with every hour that passed. He held me when I had a shitty dream, murmuring soft, sweet words to me until the dream was nothing more than an uncomfortable memory, but I could tell his mind was on the things I'd asked him not to do.

His ex-pack had asked Mare two more times if she had determined a punishment, and both times, she answered that she was still deciding.

When the sun set on the third day, we finally heard the cave's makeshift doors move.

Priel spared enough time to growl at me that I needed to *stay right there*, before he and Ervo were jogging toward the opening.

Both men were on fire.

Mare and I exchanged nervous expressions as we stood.

Out of the corner of my eye, I noticed the pack of hounds begin moving toward us.

I nudged her arm, tilting my head toward them, and her attention spun to them.

"What are you doing?" she demanded, her voice sharp.

She was always the nicest of us in the Stronghold, so I liked hearing her get angry. It made me feel more normal.

"Protecting you," one of the hounds said, his voice low as the line of them wrapped around us.

"If you won't end us, we'll serve you until we've paid off our debt," another of the men said, his fists clenching at his sides as he stared out at the pair of Wild Hunt guys waiting in front of Clevv's cave.

"How long do you have to serve to pay off a debt that you want me to kill you for?" Mare protested.

"Eternally." The hounds' solemn response would've made me laugh if it was anything but serious.

Unfortunately, it was honest.

Mare and I exchanged wide-eye glances, and then she grabbed my arm, holding on tightly.

We peered around the hounds as Clevv yelled, "I wish to make amends."

Amends?

Was he serious?

We were definitely past that, given the fact that he'd hurt Mare and abducted me.

Just in case it came to a fight, I shifted forms. Fire and smoke trailed off of my body, and I stepped in front of Mare.

"Fine. Come out and talk," Priel called down into the cave.

If he'd already removed the final door enough, I was pretty sure they would've just jumped down and murdered the guy.

"I need something as a sign of good will," Clevv added.

"Get out now or I'll kill you where you stand," my hound snarled.

A moment passed, and then Ervo and Priel were stepping back so Clevv could get out.

If they actually let him live after hurting Mare, I was honestly going to question everything I'd learned about the fae. I wasn't passionate about death sentences, but they had made it very clear that any mistreatment of women was an offense that would result in death.

As far as I knew, it had never happened before.

But as Priel had so helpfully pointed out, they weren't innocent. Clevv had known exactly what he was doing, and still decided to do it.

Clevv stood straight and confident, even as he looked at Priel and said simply, "I made a mistake."

I scoffed.

Like hell he had.

That bastard *chose* to hurt Mare.

There was a tense pause before Priel growled to Ervo, "Your female was the injured one. This is your call, Brother."

I knew what was coming, then, with a chill that slid down my spine.

In a smooth motion, too fast for my eyes to even really track, Ervo's massive body spun and swung. His claws sliced through the hound's throat faster than Clevv could so much as flinch.

And I was really damn glad that guy was on our side.

My eyes closed before I could see Clevv's head plummeting toward the ground.

I still heard the awful thunk, though.

Mare's stomach made an awful sound.

I spun to face her, shifting back to my human form as I did, and grabbed her tangled curls to hold them away from her face as she bent over and vomited. When her stomach was empty, she murmured a thank you to me, and I released her hair.

"And the other hounds?" Ervo asked Priel in a steady voice.

Priel growled again, "Still your call. My female wasn't injured because of their decisions; yours was. If you find any of these bastards responsible for the pain Mare suffered, they deserve to die as well."

Ervo studied the hellhounds forming a divider between him and us.

And then he began stalking toward us.

Mare scrambled back to her feet and shoved her way between the men, placing herself directly in front of Ervo.

He stopped a few inches from her.

"Please don't hurt them," she said.

His eyes narrowed.

"They made a mistake; that's all. If they were okay with what Clevv did, they would've kept working with him. Instead, they helped us."

Fury bloomed in his eyes.

Fuck.

Mare must've seen it too, because she sank to her knees. *"Please,* Ervo."

He grabbed her by the waist, lifting her up and setting her back on her feet. When she was steady, he released her, still glaring at her with all that damn fury.

"You are far too important to ever *kneel* for a man." His voice was barely-controlled chaos. "If you wish the hounds to live, I'll allow it. Should they ever so much as look at you wrong, I will relish their deaths. Understand?"

Mare jerked her head in a quick, rough nod.

Ervo stepped back, his gaze lifting to the row of hellhounds. I saw her shoulders sag, like she was letting out a breath of air that she'd thought she needed to hold.

But the warning glare he turned on the hounds was enough to scare me into submission, that was for sure.

"We need to meet up with the others, to make sure their females are alright," Ervo said to Priel, when he finally stepped back and removed his gaze from the hounds.

"I won't risk taking North near them until we've solidified the bond," Priel said, his eyes sweeping quickly over the group of hellhounds too.

Whether or not he was changing his mind about letting Mare decide if any of them needed to die, I didn't know.

"I understand. You'll head to your mountain?"

"We will. Don't bring any assholes to us this time, or you'll have a *real* fight on your hands," he grumbled to the phoenix. "And my head isn't so easily removed." My hound pushed two of his ex-packmates apart so he could get through their barrier and to my side. His arms went around me, and he hauled me up against his chest like I was a damn toddler.

I didn't mind it, though.

"I'll be prepared to end anyone who so much as looks at my female now," Ervo said calmly.

"As you should. If you see Lian, tell him where to find us."

"I will."

The men nodded at each other.

I flashed Mare a quick eye-roll, and she gave me a smile that didn't reach her eyes.

And in the blink of an eye, Priel tossed me onto his back as he shifted. My fingers tangled in his fur and I buried my face against the back of his neck just as he took off running.

The speed he moved at would've been more than enough to make me dizzy if I'd been human, but I wasn't human.

I was fae.

A hellhound.

A damned oracle, too.

Pride and hope swelled in my chest as Priel continued to run.

Everything was going to be okay.

I felt that *and* trusted it, for the first time since I'd been dragged into Vevol.

. . .

WE REACHED Priel's mountain a few hours later. He ran up a well-traveled path that wove halfway up the massive mountain, and when we reached the end of the trail, he shifted forms.

His arm wrapped around my waist as he set me on my feet.

"It's easier to get through in your skin," he explained to me, his lips brushing my forehead before he set my hands on his waist and then began leading me inside.

I followed closely, holding on from behind as we slid through a tight crack in the stone, and then walked along a skinny hallway that slanted downward as we walked. A few minutes later, we turned the corner, and stepped into a large cavern that made my lips part.

The ceiling was tall and wide, with stalactites shaped like water droplets seemingly dripping toward the living space. They shimmered in many different neutral colors, and made the whole damn room feel fancy.

Stalagmites bordered the expansive room as well, shaped similarly to the ones coming off of the ceiling, but stretching upward.

As far as the space's contents, it was incredible. One side of the room held a large, bubbling pool of steaming water. Another side held a huge kitchen, with a walk-in pantry missing a door so I could see right into it. Against the third wall was a gigantic shower with just one thick, clear-glass wall, and a door leading into what I assumed was the rest of the bathroom. To the side of that, a gigantic mattress was set up.

The center of the space possessed couches, fae bean bags, and chairs, clearly designed for comfort.

The final wall, which we were standing right up against, was a massive stretch of paintings. Mural, after mural, after mural, coated the wall with Priel's gorgeous landscapes, all of them featuring a small-looking hellhound.

I noticed a slight discoloration on its back leg, and then noticed a few other similar ones.

My eyes widened when I realized what they were.

Brands.

The small hellhound was me.

My gaze jerked toward Priel.

He gave me a heart-stopping grin. "You're not the only one who dreams, Gorgeous. I thought you just had unique fur. Unlike yours, mine weren't visions. Just my imagination tangling with Vevol's magic to show me the female I knew deep down was supposed to be mine."

I opened my mouth, but then closed it when I realized I didn't know what to say to that.

It was overwhelming, but in an absolutely incredible way.

He brushed a kiss against my forehead. He'd taken to doing that often, and I loved it more than I could've even imagined.

My gaze caught on another doorless closet off to the side, and happiness swelled within me when I saw the assload of both paint and books within. Priel hadn't brought them there for me, but I knew they would be mine, too.

"Well?" He squeezed my hip, and I realized he'd wrapped his arm around my waist again while I was checking out his house.

"It's perfect," I admitted.

And as I looked closer, I realized it was the same place I'd seen bits and pieces of in my dreams.

That realization made everything feel much, much more settled.

And right.

Really, really right.

"Good." He scooped me up off the ground and hauled me toward the bed.

"What are we doing?" I asked him.

"Sleeping," he grumbled.

"You sound really excited about that," I drawled back.

"I'd rather we get naked together, but I don't trust myself to stay in control while I'm this tired," he admitted.

Control?

That was what he was worried about?

I bit back a snort.

He set me on the bed.

I didn't waste any time; just grabbed the hem of my tank top and stripped it over my head.

Priel halted where he was, his gaze dropping to my tits as I tossed the fabric to the ground.

I stood up just long enough to remove my shorts, then collapsed to the mattress with a groan.

Shit, it was really comfortable.

"Everything's fireproof in here, right?" I asked, as I climbed deeper into the bed.

He was still staring at me.

His jaw was clenched now, though, and there was indecision on his face.

"Priel?" I checked.

He blinked a couple times. "Yeah?"

"You didn't answer my question."

His eyes met mine.

There wasn't a chance he had even heard the question, and I was immensely satisfied by that.

At some point over the last few days, I had stopped doubting him when he called me Gorgeous. And I *loved* that feeling.

"Everything's fireproof in here, right?" I repeated.

"Of course."

His hands slid into his pockets.

I didn't let myself stare at the bulge in his shorts, even though I wanted to.

"We don't have to do anything tonight if you're not ready, but it would be nice to have you in this bed, with all that bare skin pressing against mine." I patted the bed beside me. "Naked cuddling. That's not illegal here, is it?"

He unbuttoned his shorts and pushed them down as an answer.

My gaze dipped to his erection, and remained as heat curled in my lower belly.

Without commenting on the way I'd stared at him, he climbed into the bed and slid under the blankets with me. His arms wrapped around my bare torso, dragging my back to his chest as he got settled on his side. His erection tucked itself between my thighs, and I bit back a groan at the thick heat of it so close to my most sensitive bits.

"You're so damn perfect," he said into my ear, as he held me close.

"Right back at ya." My eyes closed as one of his gigantic hands wrapped around one of my tits. He didn't squeeze or play with it, but just held it.

I wiggled a bit, earning a few quiet growls, but he made no move to heat things up between us.

And after a few minutes passed, I realized that I was actually pretty exhausted.

My eyes eventually closed, and I fell asleep wrapped in Priel's gloriously-warm, bare skin.

MY BACK ARCHED as his tongue stroked my clit, and a desperate cry escaped me. My hands were tied above my head, my ass hanging off the edge of the bed as Priel devoured me. His fingers dug into my skin, his hands holding my thighs almost too far apart.

I needed more.

I wanted him inside me.

Two of his fingers filled me, and I clenched around them, the pleasure growing hotter and stronger.

A third finger slowly pierced my back entrance, and I lost it.

The orgasm wasn't the end, though.

One was never enough for my hellhound; my mate.

He slowed down for a minute, his tongue sliding down, and down, and—

My thoughts pierced the vision, making the moment hazy.

This wasn't what I wanted.

I didn't want to see Priel making love to me before I lived the moment; I wanted to be *in* the moment.

I wanted to feel him inside me, to watch him touch me me.

Not to dream about it, but to live it.

· · ·

As if that one thought was enough, I slid out of the vision and woke up sucking in air, blinking sleep from my eyes.

I stared out at the dark cave around me. With the way my sight worked, I wouldn't have seen any better even if there had been lights to turn on.

My body was hot, and I could feel slickness between my thighs.

Priel's breathing was even behind me, though, his grip on my breast just as relaxed as the rest of him.

He needed sleep. That was the whole reason he'd taken me away from the Stronghold in the first place, after all. He'd had time to recover since then, but more shit had gone down.

And...

I didn't think there was a chance in hell that I'd be able to fall back asleep while this horny.

Maneuvering my hand out from where he'd trapped it against my abdomen took a minute, but I let out a relieved breath when I'd freed it.

Parting my legs as much as possible, I slid my hand between my thighs.

A soft groan escaped me when I started to work out the pressure, my hips rocking just slightly. I didn't let myself move too much, not wanting to wake up Priel, but there was no way to stay completely still.

My breathing picked up as I neared the edge.

A gigantic hand tightened around my breast, squeezing it, and a cry escaped me as I shattered. I'd never been able to give myself a big orgasm, like Priel had given me, but it was a hell of a lot better than nothing.

"What the *hell* are you doing?" My hound's groggy voice was in my ear, and he sounded pissed.

"Couldn't sleep," I managed, between deep breaths.

His hand left my breast and slid between my thighs. I inhaled sharply as his long, thick fingers delved between my folds, feeling how soaked I was.

His low growl vibrated against my back. "You'd better not have gotten yourself off while I was sleeping."

My toes curled at the fury in his voice. "Why?"

"Every damn ounce of your pleasure belongs to me, Gorgeous. You steal that from me, and there are going to be consequences."

Okay, I was dripping.

"What kind of consequences?"

His fingers began stroking my clit, the movements slow but the pressure hard enough to make me see stars.

I'd seen the bastard punish me in my dreams. His hands, smacking my ass. His cock, in my throat.

And shit, he could punish me any time he wanted.

"The kind where I tie you to our bed and refuse to let you shatter until you're *begging*." His snarl and the brutal strokes of his fingers made it hard to think straight. "The kind where I fuck you hard, without giving you time to adjust. The kind where I make you *scream* while my cock is between those hot little lips."

Yeah, now the bastard was speaking my language.

And I was *really damn grateful* that Lian had shared how sex worked with my hellhound, so I didn't have to.

"Well I already got myself off while you were sleeping," I breathed. "What are you going to do about it?"

A growl escaped him, and I heard the sexy playfulness behind it.

This was a game for both of us.

"Get on your hands and knees."

I was only too eager to obey.

My ass was up in the air a heartbeat later, my body spread wide for the man I wanted so badly it hurt.

"You don't get my tongue since you decided to warm yourself up," he growled, spreading my ass wide so he could see every inch of me.

"That's fair." My body throbbed at the snarl of approval I earned, and I sucked in a breath when the head of his cock met my entrance.

"You ready, Gorgeous?" Despite the growly playfulness, I knew he'd never do anything to me that I didn't want. And ultimately, he knew this was going to be my first time.

"Fuck, yes," I breathed.

One of his hands was on my ass, the other on my thigh, as he slid his cock inside me.

My lips parted in a silent cry, my eyes closing as I took him deeper and deeper and deeper.

There was a moment of sharp pain, and then he was driving home, bottoming out within me.

His fingers dragged over my clit, and I cried out as my body struggled to adjust to his thickness. He panted and swore, remaining still as he stroked me, bringing me pleasure even as I tried to breathe and adapt.

The pressure of him inside me slowly went from uncomfortable to really damn incredible as my tension faded.

"Not going to last long," he said to me, through gritted teeth.

"We'll go again after," I panted back, earning a pinch to my clit.

He pulled out just a little, then drove home again, earning a cry.

Everything inside me swelled—and then unraveled. I felt something click between us, something thick, heady, and magical.

I cried out as I rocked my hips, making Priel roar as he followed me over the edge. The pleasure was brutal and sweet at the same time, and when I collapsed, he dragged me into his arms and held me.

"Fuck, Gorgeous," he panted alongside me, our slightly-sweaty bodies plastered together.

Mental pictures of my bare ass in the air while my body swallowed his massive cock blasted through my mind.

I remembered what January had said about the bond—that they could communicate mentally.

Shit.

If Priel was going to hit me with pictures like that, I didn't know if I'd ever be able to leave his cave.

"Wow." I held my eyes closed, hoping everything would stop spinning and his steamy thoughts would slow down. Thinking of January had reminded me about her pregnancy—and the consequences that could follow what we'd just done. "We need to find that plant. I should've thought things through more."

"It took her half a year to get pregnant, even while having sex every day," Priel said, stroking one of my nipples. "Once wouldn't be enough to do it."

"Everyone's body works differently. We have no way of knowing," I murmured back.

"Then I'll find us that damn plant before I take you again." His growl was somewhere between amused and horny.

More of those images flashed in my mind.

My ass, in his palms.

His cock, driving into my entrance.

"You're going to kill me if you keep thinking like that," I groaned.

The images cut off, though he did give me a growly chuckle. "It's going to be a long time before I can think about anything else, Gorgeous. Get used to it."

I heaved a sigh at the idea of getting out of bed when I was this horny again already. "Let's go get the plant, then."

Sixteen

We put our clothes back on, and then Priel showed me how to get back outside of the cave. His lesson on tapping into Vevol's magic to discover things about plants was sketchy at best, but it was actually pretty simple. I had to rely on following my feelings, which was difficult at first, but I figured it out.

The plant to suppress fertility was a small red ball-shaped fruit with odd protrusions on the thick, fuzzy skin. They grew on trees in mass quantities, which seemed like a good thing to me. Priel taught me how to eat it as we walked back to the cave, and as he did, the fruit reminded me of an orange. The fuzzy skin needed to be peeled off—he warned me it would make me sick if I tried to eat it. Inside, the fruit was soft but creamy, with thin membranes that made it easy to take apart like an orange was.

I groaned at the flavor when I tasted it; the sweetness and texture reminded me of ice cream, even though it wasn't cold.

I'd definitely need to stick them in the fridge, or maybe talk Priel into figuring out a way to build a freezer so I could have them like actual ice cream.

If we were going to be having a lot of sex, I would have the perfect excuse to eat a lot of them.

"Why didn't anyone ever bring these to us?" I asked Priel.

He gave me a sheepish grin. "One of the fae noticed many years ago that eating the fruit changes the thickness of our release. Word spread, and no one has touched them since." He gestured to his dick, and I realized he was talking about jizz.

Right.

Interesting.

If it changed *that*, it probably affected male fertility too, which was awesome.

"So it would stop me from getting pregnant, *and* you from getting me pregnant. Double protection. Good; we are *not* having a kid soon." I handed him one of the fruits I was cradling in the crook of my arm. "Eat it, or I'm not participating in the fantasy you keep mentally-flashing me."

He snorted, but accepted the fruit and began peeling it. "So you don't want kids?"

I glanced at him sideways. "I don't know what I want; I'm not even used to living in Vevol yet. If that was going to be a deal-breaker, you probably should've asked before we did the deed."

He flashed me an amused smirk. "You think I could only want you because you can make me a baby, Gorgeous?"

I shrugged. "I don't think so, but we've never talked about it."

"Our world is still a mess right now. Bringing a small life into it would be terrifying. What if it was a girl, like January said? Can you even imagine how many men I'd have to protect her from?" He shuddered. "There's been so damn much fighting. And I enjoy the fighting, usually. But at this point, I'd like to spend at least the next decade at home with you.

"Doing what?" I asked.

"Painting. Fucking. Inking that gorgeous skin. Teaching you about our world. You've seen so little of it, and it's an incredible place. You deserve to understand who and what you are now, Polaris, and to have as much time as you need to figure out how your magic works, to prevent it from having so much power over you."

My lips curved upward. "That sounds perfect. We'll reevaluate the kid thing in a decade."

"Or two," he agreed.

My smile widened further.

We ate as we walked back, our hips bumping against each other. Soft, comfortable electric zaps zipped between us with each small brush of our skin. Honestly, I felt so much more relaxed with him that it was almost ridiculous. Finally working through that tension and settling the connection between us made things feel so much more comfortable, even though I was totally horny.

And the electricity connecting us only served to calm me further, as if his body was telling mine that I was safe and he would take care of me.

I'd like to say that I didn't *need* him to take care of me, but honestly, I did. I was a hurricane on my best days, and I needed an anchor. Priel was uniquely qualified to fill that position, because he got it. He understood my drive to create art when my emotions grew too strong. He wasn't offended when I got angry with him, and didn't let me walk all over him—nor did I let him walk all over me.

And he understood how difficult my magic was for me. Rather than hating it the way I did for so long, he talked about my dreams as if they were something incredible.

All of those things worked together to create a man who made my future seem bright in a way it never had on Earth.

And I loved that.

WHEN WE REACHED the cave again, we stored the fruits in Priel's fae-style fridge. I grabbed a glass from the cupboard and filled it with water, leaning up against the cabinets and sipping at it while Priel stepped into the pantry and surveyed the contents.

"How long could we survive here without leaving?" I checked, when he stepped back out.

"A couple of years." He shrugged a shoulder. "Longer, if the connection truly nourishes us when it staves off our hunger."

Damn.

Maybe that shouldn't have made me feel safer, but it did.

"Thank you," I said, setting my cup down on the counter.

"For what?" He lifted an eyebrow, walking up to me and stopping when his pelvis met my abdomen.

"Getting all this ready. I know you didn't do it for me, but being able to come here, and see all of this paint, and know that I'm safe..." I bit my lip. "It means a lot to me. Things haven't been easy since I was brought here, but I feel like that's changing. And I'm really, really excited about that change."

"Good." He captured my face between his palms and lowered his lips to mine. The kiss was soft, and slow, and blissfully sweet.

"I have a request," he murmured against my mouth a few minutes later.

"What is it?" I grumbled, wanting the kiss to resume.

"I want to give you a tattoo."

My eyebrows lifted and I leaned away, the kissing suddenly forgotten. "I've always wanted one. Or fifty. Is this a claiming thing, though? Like you want to mark me as yours?"

"It is." He recaptured my lips.

I was pretty sure he was trying to soften me up, but honestly didn't mind. His kisses weren't going to make me any more likely to agree than I already was.

"What kind of tattoo?" I asked when I pulled away.

"I figured we could choose together."

He brushed his lips over my nose, and my face wrinkled at the playful kiss.

His soft chuckle made me smile a little, though.

"So you'd get the same tattoo? Or I could choose one for you too?"

"Yes." His hands slid down my arms, then the curve of my waist, before stopping to rest on my hips.

"Okay. Humans usually wear rings, on this finger." I flashed him the fourth finger on my left hand. "Some people do the middle finger, or the other hand, but I almost always saw the fourth on the left. I've seen pictures of people using tattoos instead. In my favorite ones, they just use the first letter of their significant other's name in cursive, sweeping across the finger." I traced an L over my ring finger to demonstrate.

"I like it." He nodded his approval.

"You have ink here already," I pointed out, picking up his hand and showing him the black shape on his finger. The larger tattoo had been designed to look like multiple vines snaking over his fingers, so the color was solid on the bottom chunk of that finger.

"I'll do it in silver. It'll stand out, and remind me of the first time you were in my home, when you accidentally stabbed yourself."

I rolled my eyes at him, but couldn't hide my grin.

He lifted my hand to his lips, pressing a kiss to my fourth finger. "Yours, I'll do in black ink."

I figured he would; the man clearly had a thing for black ink, and I was definitely on board with it.

"Alright. What was the tattoo you were imagining?" I checked. "What would be your ideal way to mark me as yours?"

"Fire, here." His knuckle brushed over my chest, directly over my heart.

I liked the idea. Flames were a huge part of my life now that I was in Vevol. Putting them over my heart would represent me, the way I was changing, and my relationship with Priel, too.

"Deal." Let's do it.

Fire burned in his eyes as he hauled me up onto the counter. "Wait here."

He disappeared into his art closet, coming back a minute later with a small box of ink and another one of the tattoo gun things I'd stabbed myself with before.

We were both quiet as he burned the gun's end, cleaning it easily.

The sex had been fun, and we were used to talking, teasing, and sassing each other. The mating bond had been building between us for so long that sealing it just felt like the next level for our relationship.

But tattoos... they were visible, and permanent.

And the moment we were about to share felt sort of sacred because of that.

"I'll show you how it works on myself, first," Priel explained to me, lifting his eyes to mine.

He was giving me an out. Making sure I knew he didn't expect me to go through with it if I didn't want to.

"Alright." I'd let him do things his way, so he knew I wasn't going to change his mind.

We were both silent as magic swelled within the room. It was so thick I could see it a little; a transparent flame-like cloud swirling around Priel.

He placed his hand on my thigh, using me as a table, then lowered the needle to his finger.

I watched in shocked interest as he used the needle to slowly cut through the air above his hand. The ink sizzled against his skin as his fire and magic worked together to slowly and permanently draw a cursive P over his finger.

I'd known he'd use a P for Polaris before he even started.

Full names were where the magic was at, after all.

It took a while, but eventually he put the gun down, and the magic in the room faded. He tensed and relaxed his fingers a few times, before putting his hand back on my thigh.

My throat swelled when I saw the long, looping silver letter on his ring finger.

"Do mine." I handed him my palm.

He chuckled softly, tilting me and the appendage a little as he set it down on the counter. A few minutes later, he began.

I watched every second of his work, transfixed by the miracle of it. He was incredible. I had no idea how he even tapped into a person's magic like that.

"Tapping into magic is easier than you think," he murmured to me, as he finished the letter and lifted his machine away from my hand.

"I doubt it."

"You've been tapping into mine since you arrived, remember? Vevol said that's how you determine whose future you see."

Oh, damn.

Right.

"I need to practice," I admitted.

"We can start with the other women. I'm sure they won't care." He lifted the gun to my chest, and then his eyes met mine. "Are you sure about this, Gorgeous?"

"Completely."

His lips curved upward just the tiniest bit, and then he was focused on my skin.

My eyes closed while he worked, and the silence was a comfortable one as he continued. He had to move my tank top down a bit, but it wasn't like I was bothered by having his hands on my skin.

The feeling was odd, since he was altering the way my magic affected my appearance a little, but it didn't bother me.

"Alright, keep your eyes closed," he warned me, as the magic faded around us.

He must've been finished with it.

I heard him put his things down, and then felt his arms as he scooped me up off the counter.

My forehead rested against his neck as he carried me to the bathroom, and his hands stroked my ass. He was hard, which made me a little warmer.

"Feet down," he warned, as he lowered me to the ground.

I obeyed, and left my eyes closed as he adjusted my hair and tank top.

"Alright, open them."

I peeked my eyes open, and they widened as I took in my reflection.

My hair was tucked behind my shoulders, between my back and Priel's front, exposing the tattoo.

It was a paintbrush, inked at a slant, with colored paint dripping off the tip. Fire blazed off of it wildly, but didn't appear to be actually burning it.

My throat swelled.

It was perfect.

A representation of me, and of Priel—and a gorgeous one.

I turned in his arms, digging my fingers into his neck as I pulled him down.

He hauled me up off the ground, wrapping my legs around his waist as he carried me back to the bed. Our mouths were pressed together as our tongues tangled and danced, our hands and bodies urging us to continue as Priel lowered me to the mattress without pausing our kiss.

His hands left my ass long enough to drag my shorts down my thighs and toss them to the side, and then do the same to his.

The thick heat of his erection pressed against my opening. I arched my hips, taking him inside me, and we groaned together as he slowly filled me.

"Fuck," he growled against my lips.

"Yeah," I breathed.

He worked my tank over my head, then threw that wherever the rest of our clothes had gone.

Lowering his tongue to my chest as our bodies slowly became one, he dragged it over the ink before focusing on one of my nipples. The attention and the feel of him inside me was so foreign, yet incredible. I was already so close to the edge that it was stupid—but I guessed the mate bond was responsible for it, at least partly.

Priel's fingers, cock, and every other damn part were responsible for the rest.

"After this, I'm going to taste you again," he told me, dragging his teeth over my nipple.

"Good plan," I panted, moving my hips as he pulled out slightly. "First, let's just—*ohh, shit.*" The last words were a hiss as he bit down on my nipple while he bottomed out inside me.

It was too much.

I shattered with a cry, and he snarled as he pumped into me faster, and harder.

I was still riding out the intense orgasm when he lost it. Fire danced off both of our skin as he stared down at me, chest heaving and eyes hot.

"You're so much better than I imagined," he growled at me.

"I'm not sure if that's a compliment or an insult," I mumbled back, my eyes half-closing.

"The biggest compliment." He eased himself up off of my body. "Do you trust me?"

I opened my eyes fully, staring at him a bit suspiciously. "Mostly."

He smirked. "Good enough."

I watched that gorgeous backside as he crossed the room, and continued watching as he opened a kitchen cupboard. When he returned to me, he was holding a small tub.

"Is that the pleasure spice?" I checked.

"Yup." He sat on the edge of the bed, his gaze wicked. "I want to take my time with you, watch you unravel a dozen times before I'm inside you again."

Who would be crazy enough to say no when they had a sexy fae offering that? One who looked like Priel and actually cared about them?

"Hell yes."

His lips curved up in a grin, and he unscrewed the lid of the tub as he climbed back onto the bed, positioning himself so his head was between my thighs.

Licking a finger, he dipped it in the spice before pressing it to my clit.

I groaned at the pressure as he slowly dragged his finger down the center of me, before dipping it back in the spice.

"Don't know if that's sanitary," I managed, as he slid the finger inside me.

My body clenched around him, my insides still drenched with both of our pleasure.

"You're a fae, Polaris. Couldn't get a disease if you tried."

He reached up to my breasts and dragged his damp, spiced finger over my nipples just as the shit began to work on my clit.

I felt the sensitive skin warm and swell slightly, and a moan slid from my lips as he blew lightly against the flesh.

He put the lid back on the spice before dropping the container on the floor and wiping his finger down the creases between my thighs.

"Not using it on yourself?" I asked him, though with the heat coursing through me, it came out sounding like a whimper.

"Hell no. I want to watch every second of your bliss. Now, wrap those little hands around the headboard, or I'll tie them there." He blew against my clit again, and I bucked my hips desperately as the first orgasm rolled through me, making me cry out.

"Shit," I moaned, my breathing staggered as I recovered. "I don't know if I can do this."

"We're just getting started, Gorgeous, and you're already perfect. Just relax and let yourself enjoy it."

I started to nod, but then his tongue found my swollen clit.

And the pleasure became all-consuming.

For a few blissful hours, the only thing on my mind was the incredible way Priel touched me and licked me.

WHEN THE SPICE finally began to wear off, I grabbed the man by the hair and tugged him up toward me.

His eyes were hot, his gaze so damn proud. Whether he was proud of himself or me, I didn't know or care.

I felt too incredible for that.

When I pushed him to his back, the fire in his eyes was searing.

And when I wrapped my lips around his cock, getting him off with my mouth before taking him inside me and making him lose control again, every shred of doubt had been wiped from my mind.

Priel was mine.

I was his.

And we were one.

No matter what else happened, that was always going to remain true.

The past wasn't going anywhere, but the future?

It was ours.

Seventeen

Lian finally showed up outside our cave a few weeks later, roaring to get us to come out.

Priel's face was between my thighs when the roar shook our mountain, my hands and tits plastered to the wall of our living room while he knelt below me, pinning my core to his face and spreading me open wide with his hands.

He growled at me that the bastard could wait outside, then dragged his teeth over my clit until I screamed.

His cock filled me in time to catch the end of my orgasm, and his fingers tortured my clit as he pumped into me until we both lost control together.

His arm wrapped around my waist, holding me up and blazing his fire over both of us to clean our skin as I panted and wheezed. He set me down on the bed, grabbing my clothes from wherever I'd lost them a few days earlier. When I tried to take them from him, he batted my hands away and dressed me himself.

I scowled at him, and earned a wicked grin in response.

He pulled a few of the red fruits out of the fridge, tucking them into his pockets before he strode back over to me and whisked me up off my feet. My head crashed into his chest, making me laugh.

He grinned down at me. "Ready to see if January and Naomi saved the world?"

"You know they didn't. My dreams are still shitty," I said with a sigh, as I relaxed into his arms. It wasn't a shock to him; he had comforted me after my nightmares too many times for that, and reassured me that he was okay with the horrific murals I'd painted over his wall as a result of said nightmares.

He understood my need to paint, and had no problem holding my brush or mixing my colors when I was overtaken by that need.

We had even discussed (at length) our silent obsessions with each other from the time before he abducted me, so there were no more secrets between us. Only friendship, and playfulness, and a hell of a lot of attraction.

"It'll take time for things to change." He brushed my hair out of my face as he carried me to the cave's exit. "Vevol won't give you permission to go after the women until she's certain that the war isn't in our future."

"What if that never happens, though?"

"Then we'll figure something out." His voice was light and playful. "I don't think it's going to come to that, though."

Shit, I hoped not.

We emerged from the cave shortly after, and found January and Calian waiting outside. January was grinning like a fool, and I couldn't help but mirror the expression.

"Look how cozy the two of you got," she teased me.

"Extremely cozy," I admitted, trying to worm my way out of Priel's arms.

He only held me tighter, shooting me a teasing grin.

"What happened with the unseelie?"

Her smile faded a bit. "It was rough. Really rough. I thought Naomi was going to murder Aeven for a bit, but he pulled through. All the other girls are moved in, and both types of fae have started building houses and shit around the new Stronghold. It's weird, but I think it's going to turn out okay. Only a few little fights have broken out, now that the Wild Hunt guys and the unseelie council have started banishing anyone who fights."

Huh.

That wasn't a bad idea at all.

"It's like juvie in there with all the unseelie chicks running around. They're kind of bad-ass, but really guarded, and bitchy too. I saved a room for you, though." She winked at me.

I made a face. "Thanks, but I think I'm gonna keep living here. I like being out of the way, far from the big groups of fae."

"I figured. The way they talk about you is kind of crazy. Like you're the chosen one." She shrugged. "No offense, but even with all that extra magic, you're still one of us human ladies."

She winked at me. Honestly, her words and playfulness made me feel good.

Hearing that I was one of them and I always would be, made me feel like I could belong with them if I wanted to, the same way I now belonged with Priel.

She added, "We're ready for you, though. The unseelies have vowed not to try to steal you away, and apparently their vows are unbreakable or something. It's time to go after the fae women."

Shit.

I hesitated.

"You're not convinced?" she asked.

"She's still dreaming about war," Priel said simply.

January's grin faded, and Lian's expression grew serious.

"Seeing the changes for yourselves and testing the unseelies' vows could help," he suggested. "They understand your connection to Vevol, and no one will force you to go before you're ready. No one is willing to risk the fae women."

I nodded. "We'll at least go and see what it's like."

"It's weird," January warned. "The unseelie chicks are a lot less sunshiney than our seelie girls."

I grimaced. "Thanks for the warning."

"Sure." She and Lian smoothly shifted while launching themselves airborne.

I watched the phoenix and dragon fly away before looking at Priel. "Do you think it'll be safe for me there?"

"I think I'll kill anyone who tries to touch you, so regardless of how safe it is, you're going to be fine."

I rolled my eyes at him, and he flashed me a grin.

"Seriously?"

"In all honestly, Gorgeous, you're the only one who knows where the women are. Other than Mare, but no one knows that but the two of us. No one will dare risk pissing you off until the other fae women have been found, and something tells me that after we've brought them back, everyone will be too distracted to notice you and I slipping out and heading back home."

I loved that our cave was home.

And honestly, I believed him.

We shifted together, taking off toward the neutral territory.

Or the *female* territory, I supposed.

HOURS PASSED before we finally made it there, but as we approached, I realized how much more chaotic it was then I had expected.

January wasn't kidding about the houses. The damn things were going up *everywhere*. Between trees, up in the branches, within the *trunks* of the largest trees...

The fae were moving in, the way humans usually did.

And as I passed them, I started to see more than just the half-naked seelies. There were unseelie fae with their icy expressions, slacks, and button-down shirts, mixed in with the seelies. All of them were building homes and staking their claim in the neutral territory.

When they saw me and Priel coming through, the seelies stared.

The unseelies bowed.

My grip on Priel's hand tightened.

He peeled my fingers out of his, placing them on his bicep so he could wrap his arm around my waist and pull me closer as we walked.

"You okay?" he murmured into my mind.

The ability had come with the mating connection, of course, we just usually didn't bother with it. It took more focus than normal speaking, so we'd never had a reason to.

Now, we did.

Not sure I had the focus to respond mentally, I just nodded.

His grip on me tightened anyway, his fingers curving possessively around the bare strip of my abdomen.

"These bastards need to stop staring at your ass," he growled at me.

Given how relaxed he'd been over the last few weeks—and how incredible said relaxation had made my life—I took it upon myself to at least try to preserve his calm attitude.

"Staring at my butt might result in death," I called out to the men around us. "Don't test my mate."

I felt Priel's thick, hot pride at the title, and fought the curve of my lips that tried to make itself seen.

Ervo swooped out of the sky, shifting and landing smoothly on my other side as we continued walking. Obviously, he kept up with my pace easily.

"It's safe?" Priel asked the other man.

Lian had already told him it was, but I knew Priel would feel more confident if more of his friends confirmed that.

"It's not safe, but your female isn't at risk." The phoenix didn't bother with a lie, which was both a good and bad thing.

"Who is, then?" I asked him.

"Any male who tries to speak with one of the unmated females." I saw the fury burn through his eyes. "The unseelie women have been told about our arrangement, and decided that it's over."

"That's not their call," Priel growled.

"No, but to challenge them is to start a fight, and fighting leads to expulsion from the females' territory. A way for men and women to interact peacefully must be created, or the fragile peace will end." Ervo's simple statement of the words made me shiver.

Was he threatening to do something drastic?

"He may not admit it aloud, but he considers Mare his. Anyone who gets between them right now will be seen as a target," Priel said into my mind. *"She needs to mate with him, tell him she isn't interested, or choose another male."*

"I'm sure she'll be thrilled about that set of options," I grumbled back.

His low chuckle made me smile.

"Fuck, is North smiling? What happened?" I heard Ana call from somewhere in the distance. When I turned my head, I saw her standing next to another girl I didn't recognize, talking to a group of other women. They were building something, or at least trying to, and a bunch of fae men watched them warily from nearby.

My smile morphed into a grimace, but I waved anyway.

Though I understood her overprotectiveness, and had sort of appreciated it at one point, she had encouraged us to be afraid of the fae. And that fear hadn't benefited any of us, in any way. Things had been so much happier at the Stronghold after the Wild Hunt started coming around, protecting us and whatnot.

The new Stronghold came into view, and I looked it up and down.

It was still made of the bland stone, and stuck out like a sore thumb compared to the natural-looking homes the fae were building in the forest around it.

A second floor had been added to the triangular building, and it had been drastically expanded. Now it was a typical square shape, and much, much larger.

Then again, there were twenty ex-human women, and only a few of us were mated. The mated unseelie ladies didn't live with their men, as far as I knew, which left eighteen grown-ass women in need of their own space and privacy.

When I considered that there was an unnumbered group of fae women hiding out there, I realized just how much more space we would need.

"Damn," Priel whistled.

"There are many more women, now," Ervo agreed, though his gaze was on one of the second-floor windows and wasn't moving.

I would've put money on that being Mare's window, if money was really a thing in Vevol. They seemed to have some version of it, but considering all the free time they all had, it didn't seem to matter much in the scheme of things.

We walked up to the door, and Ervo knocked.

"Walking in without permission is supposed to result in castration for male fae," he told us, his voice low. "It has yet to happen, though."

I rolled my eyes.

No way in hell was anyone actually cutting anyone else's balls off. Even Ana wasn't that crazy.

A girl I didn't recognize opened the door, her eyes narrowed and suspicious as she looked at me. "North?" she checked.

"Yup."

"Men stay outside. House rule." She pointed to a couple chairs someone had set up outside.

Priel scoffed. "Not a fucking chance."

I narrowed my eyes back at the woman, muttering silently for Priel to let me handle this.

If men had dick-measuring contests, women had tit-measuring ones. And I might not have had the biggest physical tits, but I'd make it work.

"My mate poses no threat to anyone here. We both come in, or I walk right the hell away with information that could make your life here *much* easier."

The more women we had, the more the male fae's attention would be divided, so I knew without a doubt that I was right.

Everyone's life would be easier with more ladies for the fae to bother.

She scowled at me but jerked the door open, her glare turning to Ervo. "Unmated men stay out."

He glowered back at her, but I shot him what I hoped was a promising expression.

I'd talk to Mare for him.

The door slammed behind us, and the girl glared at me for a long moment. "Where the hell have you been?"

"Relieving stress with my mate; thanks for asking. You look like you could use a little *stress relief* yourself," I drawled back.

She spun around and stormed away, her brown curls bouncing behind her as she moved.

I glanced up at Priel to make sure he wasn't checking out her ass or anything, but he was already grinning down at me. *"You're sexy when you're mean."*

"Keep it in your pants until we're out of the shark tank," I murmured back, squeezing his bicep tightly.

Ervo had been staring at the second floor, so it was safe to assume that was where I would find Mare, and hopefully Sunny and Dots too.

His chuckle made me grin as we headed toward the staircase off to my left. The place honestly still looked almost as cold and unwelcoming as it had been before they expanded it and added furniture. The living room and kitchen were set up almost exactly the same way they had been back in the old Stronghold, but the space lacked life. No one was down there, watching a movie, reading a book, or even cooking.

We climbed the stairs while still holding on to each other. At the top, I looked around.

All I could see was another long, cold hallway, and two rows of doors.

"Damn," I whispered.

"Hmm?" Priel looked at me.

"It just feels empty and angry in here. Back at the Stronghold, it was a family. I was the pissed-off black sheep, but I still knew I was welcome," I explained quietly.

Looking around, I debated knocking on doors but just decided to go with the seelie way of locating people.

"Mare?" I called out. "Sunny? Dots?"

"In here!" Sunny yelled from the door furthest from the staircase.

Dots opened it a few seconds later, as we headed their way.

"Hey!" She threw her arms around me for a quick hug. "Come on in." When she grabbed my hand and tugged, Priel and I let her pull us inside.

My eyebrows shot upward when I saw three mattresses staggered around the room. It wasn't a big room, so there wasn't a whole lot of space. Between each of them, there was only four or five inches.

Mare was curled up on the bed in the corner nearest to the window, her thighs to her chest and a book resting against her knees. She gave us a faint smile before returning her eyes to the pages.

Sunny was sprawled out on the mattress in the opposite corner of Mare's, but she was sitting up and grinning at us. "Look at the two of you, all matey and cozy."

I snorted, and Dots laughed.

"What are you all doing in here?" I asked, letting go of Priel's arm. He leaned up against the wall, releasing his grip on me so I could go over to them and plop down on the end of Sunny's mattress.

"Hiding from the unseelie chicks," Sunny admitted.

I frowned.

"Not hiding," Dots corrected. "We're just... avoiding them."

"AKA hiding," Sunny agreed.

"They're not very friendly," Dots admitted. "When you do talk to them, they just go on and on about how much they hate the fae. They're hoping you can find enough fae chicks to distract all of the men. Even the mated ones."

My eyebrows shot upward.

I'd seen and heard enough of Priel's thoughts to know that wasn't even almost a possibility. Mated fae were completely devoted to their mate, even if they didn't show that. Ervo and Mare weren't even fully mated yet, but I'd seen him out there. Someone was going to die if he didn't see her soon.

Priel snorted. "Pipe dream."

"We think so too," Dots agreed.

"What happened to the Wild Hunt guys?" I checked.

Dots' and Sunny's expressions both soured. "The other girls scared them off. That's why Sunny's moping. Teris wouldn't ever agree to bang her, and now she can't even make out with him."

"I'm going to kill you," Sunny muttered, smacking Dots on the arm lightly.

"Then you won't have anyone to snuggle with," she pointed out.

Sunny groaned. "We need to get back to the old Stronghold. Things were better there."

"Until we were attacked and abducted," Mare muttered.

"Right. Until that." Sunny pointed a finger gun in her direction. "Any ideas how we can avoid that happening again?" She looked at me.

I shrugged. "Stay here?"

Priel spoke up from the side of the room. "Now that we know it's a possibility, my brothers will be going through our people, ensuring that none of you are in danger. Both Nev and Ervo are watching the house right now, and I saw Teris run out to meet January and Lian when they landed a few minutes ago." He gestured toward the window. "You're safe."

"But trapped," Sunny pointed out. "And lonely."

"We'll figure out a way to meet up with the guys," Dots protested. "The girls won't let us do movie nights or anything with them, but we can always go out there."

"About that..." I tucked some hair behind my ear. "Have the other girls come up with a way for everyone to interact safely with the men?"

Sunny snorted. "These chicks, interacting politely with fae dudes? That's never going to happen."

Dots' grimace confirmed that.

I admitted, "I have it on good authority that if we can't amend that, the war is going to break out one way or another."

No need to tell them that Ervo was the said good authority, right?

"Also, Mare, Ervo seems a little unhinged. Can you just open a window to smile and wave at him or something so he knows you're alive and well?"

"The windows are sealed shut," Mare murmured, not looking up from her book.

"Seriously?" I looked at Sunny and Dots.

Dots nodded.

"Who's in charge?" I asked them.

"There's a gang of them. Five chicks. They're the loudest." Dots made a face.

"No wonder January said it's like juvie." I glanced toward the door.

I was suddenly understanding why I was still having dreams about war.

There was a moment of tense silence as I considered our options.

What was there, really?

The men weren't a danger to each other anymore, but the damn place was going to implode if the women didn't change their ways.

Or... if the number of women didn't increase.

Vevol had given me the information. Technically, it should be my call as to when we went after them.

I didn't feel great about it, but didn't see another option, either.

"I think getting the other women will be our best way to delay the fighting," I admitted. "This place is a mess, but it's going to take longer to get it sorted out than I think we have to do so."

"Agreed," Sunny muttered.

"So, are you guys coming on that trip?" I checked. "I don't trust any of the unseelie chicks, and women are the only ones who can cross into the fae ladies' hiding place, so I need you. No way in hell will Lian let January run into the unknown while growing a baby."

Sunny sat up, excitement in her eyes. "I'm so down. The Wild Hunt dudes taught us how to shift while we waited to hear back about this place, so we're golden."

Dots grimaced, but nodded.

Mare finally put her book away. "I want to see them, too."

"Alright, let's get out of here." I stood up.

Maybe it would've been smarter to wait a few days before taking off, but I didn't want to risk any of the unseelie ladies trying to talk their way into the group.

Honestly, there was a decent chance the lot of them would want to go there just to hide out from the men.

Priel and I waited in the hallway while the other girls all put on their seelie tanks and shorts, or stripped down to them.

"I'm surprised the other ladies are so bitter," I murmured to Priel, as he pulled me closer and played with a few strands of my hair.

"I'm not."

I rolled my eyes at him.

He flashed me a grin. "Things were rough at first, Gorgeous. We'll figure out a way to make this work, but it'll take time."

"If only we had more of that." My mind went back to my dreams.

"Soon enough, it'll be just the two of us, relaxing in the hot spring back at home," he murmured to me. "Enjoy the wild times while they last."

The doors opened, and all three of the girls stepped out.

Emotions I couldn't identify swelled in my chest when I saw all of them wearing the same simple tanks and shorts I had on.

Modest, we were not.

But united?

Hell yes.

Eighteen

THE GIRL from earlier tried to prevent us from leaving, the same way she'd tried to prevent me from coming inside. I threatened to punch her in the face, and she moved.

January's juvy theory was only getting more and more accurate.

It felt like a million eyes were on us as we stepped out of the new Stronghold together.

As if we'd summoned them, Nev and Ervo came strolling out of the forest and joined the group.

"We're going after the female fae," Priel announced, his voice booming into the forest. "Follow us, and you die. Seelie or unseelie, we don't care."

With that, he tossed me over his shoulder and shifted.

I grinned at the rush of the familiar motion. It was stupid, but I loved the way he threw me around like that.

I loved a lot of things about Priel, actually.

The others shifted too, and as a group, we took off. Calian and January met Ervo, Mare, and Dots in the sky while the rest of us moved on the ground. Teris caught up to us, running too.

I'd never seen the basilisks or how they moved while up close and personal, but they were fascinating. And strangely, not as creepy as I'd thought. Thicker around than me or Priel, they were absolutely massive, their bodies built out of pure muscle. Despite their size, they moved just as quickly as the rest of us, their bodies zigging and zagging smoothly.

A BIT of time passed before Priel growled at me. *"Do you hear that?"*

I frowned. *"Hear what?"*

"Someone's followed us. I need you to shift and run while I take care of it."

I growled back, *"By yourself? No way."*

"I'll be fine. Teris or Nev will break away to help, too."

I stared out at the forest as we ran, moving insanely fast. Though memories of the awful way I'd hit the ground when I jumped out of that car assaulted me, I pushed them away.

I wasn't the same weak human girl.

I was strong, now.

I could do this.

Starting the shift, I threw myself off of Priel's back.

All four of my paws hit the ground, and victory coursed through my veins.

"That's right," Priel growled back at me, his voice somewhere between satisfied and proud. *"You're incredible, Gorgeous. Now stay with the rest of the pack, so I don't have to spank that sexy little ass when we stop."*

I huffed out a snort, shaking my head at my mate and his steamy playfulness as he darted in the wrong direction.

Sure enough, Nev broke away from the group too.

Teris remained on the opposite side from me, protecting Sunny's scaly side. I noticed Lian fly lower, as if also responding to the threat, getting ready to protect the rest of us if we needed him to.

My heart swelled at the sight.

We were a damn family.

Snarls erupted behind me, and I tried to look over my shoulder, but didn't see anything.

A few minutes later, a whole group of hellhounds caught up with us.

My surprised gaze flickered over each of them as recognition kicked in.

They were Priel's ex-pack.

"They still owe Mare their lives," Priel growled to me, as he caught back up to us. *"The bastards aren't leaving unless we kill*

them, and considering Mare ended up on her knees to stop Ervo from ripping their throats out, that's not an option."

"Damn," I murmured, glancing up at the sky.

Mare didn't seem like herself, but at least she had protection.

"Well, this has been quite an interesting day," I finally said.

Priel's chuckle made me grin. *"One of many, I imagine."*

My heart warmed. *"I'm in love with you,"* I told him, not wanting to keep it quiet.

He loved me too; I didn't doubt that.

"If you're trying to seduce me, it's working," he rumbled back.

A barked laugh escaped me.

"I love you too, Polaris. So damn much." His voice was warm, and I moved closer to his side. Our fur brushed as we ran, and as the sun set over our heads, I admitted to myself that I was happy.

Stupidly, ridiculously happy.

And no matter what we were going to face next, I refused to let that change.

NINETEEN
PRIEL

WE STOPPED for the night when we reached the lake. None of us men were willing to watch our women fly into the darkness to go after the female fae; they could wait until the sun was up so we could at least see where they disappeared at and figure out a way to go after them if we needed to.

I trusted North's magic enough not to think that would be necessary, but some of the others weren't as certain.

And I wanted to spend the night with her first, in case the trip took a few days. I despised the thought of having my female away from me for any amount of time, but there might not be a way around it.

For the sake of peace, I would survive it. Not happily, but survival was survival.

Sunny, Dots, and Mare all made their beds together, with their men nearby, watching them. Sunny invited Teris to share her blankets, but the moron turned her down.

Why he would turn down the female he'd claimed when she clearly wanted him was beyond me, but I sure as hell wasn't getting involved.

Lian and January went off together, and North grabbed my hand, drawing me away from everyone else too.

She was exhausted, so when she collapsed into my arms, I simply stroked her back, enjoying her presence.

There would be time for sex later.

Plenty of time.

An eternity.

That thought made my lips curve upward.

I drifted off to sleep quickly too, and didn't wake up until North was shaking my shoulders, positioned over me with bright, excited eyes.

"I saw the future," she told me, a bit breathless. "A *happy* future, Priel. There were kids, running around. Unseelies were *smiling*. I was right; we made the right choice."

"Of course you were right." I pulled her face down to mine, kissing her gently.

"I know you didn't doubt me, but I doubted me. And there were so many nightmares…" she shivered. "I don't think I can sleep right now. I'm too excited."

"Need me to relax you?" I murmured, sliding my hands down to her perfect little ass and squeezing lightly.

Her eyes dilated a bit, and she looked at the trees around us.
"Here?"

"Why not?" My fingers slid beneath the hem of her shorts.
"Make sure you're loud enough that the other men know how
good I am at pleasuring you."

She laughed, until I dragged a finger over her clit.

Then, she shuddered.

And as I made love to her on the floor of the forest, I knew
without a shadow of doubt that I was the luckiest male in our
world.

Hell, the luckiest male in *all* the worlds.

EPILOGUE
MARE

I STARED out at the lake, watching Vevol's sun rise slowly over the body of water. I'd thought it was an ocean until a few weeks ago, honestly.

A man stepped into place beside me.

I didn't have to turn my head to know which one. The group of hellhounds that thought they were my protectors never came this close to me.

And the only unmated man who did was a certain possessive, confusing-as-hell phoenix.

"You should remain here while the others go," he said to me, his voice even.

His voice was always so even, unless he was cutting someone's head off.

I fought the horrified shiver that threatened to roll down my spine with the memories that accompanied that thought.

The way the head had fallen...

The uncaring, unfeeling look in Ervo's eyes...

My stomach's contents threatened to make a reappearance.

It wouldn't be the first time I vomited at the memory. Nor would it likely be the last.

"Why would I do that?" I tried to keep my voice as level as his.

Maybe if I refused to let him see what I was feeling, his possessiveness would fade, and the confusing emotions it made me feel would too.

He had made it very clear that despite his constant reminders that I belonged to him, he thought I belonged to him as nothing more than a family member.

A female brother, he had said.

My lips twisted at the unpleasantness of the memory.

That conversation had left me so confused.

"You'll be safer here," he said.

"I stopped caring about my safety a long time ago." I stared out at the water.

How many years had I spent hoping for a second chance to be someone bigger, and stronger, and better?

My whole damn life.

I wanted to *matter*.

And this was my chance. Hopefully, the first of many.

"Precisely why you should remain here. The group doesn't need someone who won't watch their own back."

I scowled at him. "My back doesn't need watching. North's does; she's the important one."

His eyes pierced mine. "Every female is important."

"Which is exactly why I'm going with the group, to attempt to retrieve the ones in hiding." I turned back to the lake, trying to calm my furiously-beating heart.

There was a long, tense moment of silence between us before Ervo spoke again.

This time, his voice was so low I barely heard it at all. "Should something happen, my full name is Viervo."

My eyes widened.

Giving someone your full name, in Vevol, gave them power over you.

No one gave out their full name.

"Vee-air-vo?" I quietly pronounced the name, trying to embed it in my memory. Admittedly, I was terrible at remembering the fae's strange names, and the pronunciations were even more difficult.

"Yes."

I swallowed roughly, still staring out at the lake. "Thanks. I'm not going to need help, though."

There was another brief moment of silence.

I felt more than saw Ervo's body slowly tensing.

"Should something happen to you, I would burn this whole fucking world down to get you back," he finally said.

The unevenness in his voice surprised me, but I tried not to show him that.

"Like a brother, right?" I drawled.

He blinked. "Of course."

I shook my head, turning and striding away before I could overthink our relationship even more than I already had.

It was time for me to move on. Life in Vevol might not have been short, but it was definitely too long to continue mooning over a man who loved me like a sister.

"Ready?" North called from across the beach.

"You have no idea," I called back.

She grinned, and I shifted forms.

It was time to change the damn world—even if said world was small, and full of people I didn't particularly like.

AFTERTHOUGHTS

What a twist.

Which twist am I referring to, you ask?

Honestly, I don't even know at this point.

I thought things were going to be all fun and games in Vevol for this book and the next. Sure, I expected a little kidnapping, thanks to the flood of desperate fae dudes outside the Stronghold. Maybe even a little torture. I didn't even expect North's paintings would actually be her seeing the future when I planned this book.

But then the first twist happened.

And the second.

And now I'm pretty sure this book was *all* twist.

Plus a few sexy times, of course ;P

Things never happen the way we want them to, in life or in stories. Shit happens. People change. Circumstances shift, and everything else that possibly can does too.

But in the end, everything always turns out okay. And sometimes, that's what gets me through the next chapter, the next day, and the next week.

Particularly when I'm drinking way too much caffeine to finish editing at 4 AM after too much anxiety and avoidance of said editing.

That's when I wax poetic, I guess.

Life, and books, are just really beautiful to me.

And I'm grateful for that.

Anyway, as always, thank you so much for reading!

All the love,

Lola Glass <3

P.S. Did you catch the not-so-sneaky reference to my Supernatural Underworld series, if you've read it? Not gonna lie, it made me a little teary-eyed. I'm thinking my other version of hellhounds might need their own standalone series sometime soon... but there are so many other books to write... who knows, man. Anything can happen!

And now I sound like a stereotypical surfer guy. Cool.

Thanks again for reading!

Free Novella

Join my email list with this link to read a free novella featuring an adorable werewolf couple you may have met in one of my other series ;)
FREE NOVELLA
You'll receive updates on book releases as well as any upcoming deals and promotions. No spam!

If you'd like to subscribe to text notifications about new releases (and only new releases), text the word BOOKS to the number (855) 293-3564

PLEASE REVIEW

Here it is. The awkward page at the end of the book where the author begs you to leave a review.
Believe me, I hate it more than you do.
But, this is me swallowing my pride and asking.
Whether you loved or hated this story, you made it this far, so please review! Your reviews play a MASSIVE role in determining whether others read my books, and ultimately, writing is a job for me—even if it's the best job ever—so I write what people are reading.
Regardless of whether you do or not, thank you so much for reading <3
-Lola

Stay in Touch

Check out my reader group, Lola's Book Lovers
for giveaways, book recommendations, and more!

Or find me on:
TIKTOK
INSTAGRAM
PINTEREST
GOODREADS

ABOUT THE AUTHOR

Lola is a book-lover with a *slight* romance obsession and a passion for love—real love. Not the flowers-and-chocolates kind of love, but the kind where two people build a relationship strong enough to last. That's the kind of relationship she loves to read about, and the kind she tries to portray in her books.

Even if they're about shifters :)

Made in the USA
Las Vegas, NV
04 February 2025

17518491R00154